Secret Death-Defying Escape Finally Told

A Novel by
Wally Wolsky

Copyright © 1995
by Wally Wolsky

All rights reserved. No part of this book, either in part or in whole, may be reproduced, transmitted or utilized in any form or by any means, electronic, photographic or mechanical, including photocopying, recording, or by any information storage and retrieval system, without permission in writing from the Publisher, except for brief quotations embodied in literary articles and reviews.

For permissions, or for serialization, condensation, or for adaptations, write the Author at P.O. Box 514, Valley City, ND 58072

International Standard Book Number: 0-942323-21-1

Edited by Donalee Josephson
Illustrations: Susan Grim

Production: Creative Media, Inc.
Design: Sheldon Larson

Published by
North American Heritage Press
A DIVISION OF
CREATIVE MEDIA, INC.
Minot, North Dakota
Printed in the United States of America

Dedication

*I dedicate this book
to my beloved son Steven,
who provided the
encouragement for me to tell
the remarkable story of
a brave and determined
group of people.*

*Steven died of Cancer
February 12th, 1993.*

*Dolores and Wally
Wolsky*

Introduction

THE SECRET that is about to be told in this book has been kept for nearly one hundred years. The escape of Germans from Russia, the Ukraine.

It is unbelievable that several thousand people could be involved in a secret, and yet it never leaked out to the public. It still could be a bit dangerous to some, but I believe it should be told so future generations may know of the sacrifices, torture, and death their forefathers endured, so we may be born in a nation such as America or Canada.

Somehow through all of this, they hung on to their faith, sanity and pride. Those with whom I have spoken about this have said it's time to let the cat out of the bag. Come out of the closet, so to speak, and tell it all.

I have put this in the form of a novel for several reasons. Mainly, I don't have to use accurate names, dates and places, so the innocent can be protected.

Regardless of your background or nationality, the story can be appreciated by everyone.

Table of Contents

CHAPTER		PAGE
1	Opportunities Of A New Land	1
2	A Brutal Winter – The Warmth Of Friendship	17
3	Establishing Themselves In The New Land	27
4	Changing Times, Unrest, Taxes	43
5	A Secret Mission	63
6	Journey To Freedom	75
7	The Ravages Of Winter	89
8	Freedom, Opportunity, Life!	101
9	German-Russians In America	113
10	A Wolsky Family Overview	121

Preface

WHAT A FIND! UNBELIEVABLE! As we peeled the third to the last twelve-inch board from the wall; a dusty brown bag-like object was stuffed between the studs in the wall. As I carefully removed it I noticed another in the next. What can this be? As I carefully opened it, we see a complete journal going back generations.

The family trees, their movements, their happy times, their sad times, the politics, and all. Also, and this is what I based my book on, a secret set of documents explaining a still-secret escape of several thousands. This is most likely the only written account in the world today.

I read far into the night and have since reread it again dozens of times. It is the kind of thing when you read, its so secret you want to close the door and lock it as you read.

I pondered a long time before I wrote this. Grandpa considered it important yet too secret to tell anyone. Did he want me or whomever found it to tell? Would people still be in jeopardy? I don't know. Would I get into trouble! I discussed this with my family and like most discussions, there were opinions favoring each way. My son, Steve, who is now dead as a result of cancer was real insistent that I do it. He felt the heirs of these people have a right to know their background and history — their roots.

This house that I'm talking about is the old, original Wolsky house which I inherited some years back from my father and even though it is nearly one hundred years old, it is in good shape. We were going to do some remodeling when I took out this wall and found this masterpiece.

I grew up next to grandpa and he told me much about our background, but he never mentioned what is in this book to me or to anyone.

Some things are not very flattering, but the truth rarely is. This involves hundreds of people whose ancestors are here in this country today.

Their disappointments, joy, sorrow, tenacity, faith, and strength, will be felt by thousands.

CHAPTER **1**

Opportunities Of A New Land

GERMANY ITSELF was comprised of unorganized states. The wars and rule of Frederick the Great had impoverished all of Germany! Their marks had been devalued; they were overtaxed; their sons had been hauled off to wars in areas in which they had no interest…By 1763 they were destitute.

The czar of Russia had married a German princess named Catherine. She knew what her country lacked, and what its people wanted and needed. She also knew her country's people were good ambitious farmers. Russia had a lot of unimproved land — good land — some of the best in the world.

The Russian farmers didn't seem to know how to break this land and make it productive. Catherine's job was to entice the impoverished Germans to immigrate to unknown, yet potentially productive, parts of Russia and solve their food problem.

She sent agents west to Germany to sell Russia to the German farmers. Germans, at that point in history, did not trust the Russians. They did not like them, and considered them uncouth slobs. Catherine made them many promises: Free land to the serfs, freedom of religion, exemption from serving in the army, freedom from taxes, low interest loans to start farming. In addition, they would each have their

Secret Death Defying Escape Finally Told

Queen Catherine of Russia (formerly a German princess) now married to the tsar of Russia. She is talking to a group of German farmers, selling them on the idea of immigrating to the Ukraine.

own acreage, and something they had never had before — no taxes for 15 years! It sounded like paradise.

Catherine sold the czar on this plan, because she told him they would integrate and become a part of Russian society. The push was on but, initially, not many takers signed on.

My story began with the first wave of Germans — a few hundred who came and moved to the Ukraine.

My family had a mercantile store, which handled a wide variety of needs from groceries to hardware to clothing. We also had a couple acres for garden ground behind the building. The vegetables were sold through the store as they ripened. It was pretty much a family operated store. Two brothers owned it together — Max and Albert Wolske. Max, was the oldest and had four children who worked around the store and did much of the gardening in the summer. Albert was newly married, but there were other cousins and family members also working there. The Wolske's also owned a small flour mill, where farmers brought wheat and exchanged it for flour and cereal. Until now, business had been good.

The German government, suffering from tremendous financial burdens, began doubling taxes and devalued their mark twice. For every mark a citizen had, it was worth only 40 percent in credit.

Can you imagine what this did to the store? What they had paid one mark for was now worth only 40 percent! They closed their doors.

If that wasn't bad enough, all of their customers were in the same shape, so they wanted to charge what they bought. Every business on main street closed!

Our family got together with some friends (most everyone was related), and carefully packed what they had in wagons — all their food and supplies. They put high wooden sides on the wagons and wood tops to keep everything dry. The top was hinged so, during the day, they could open them and play checkers or cards. One wagon was strictly for cooking. One man was named head cook, and the rest took turns helping and doing kitchen chores.

The laundry was handled in the same way. They stopped and washed in streams. The wagon team that headed east was quite a sight. They were not too uncomfortable; traveling in wagons was the only mode of transportation they knew, so they didn't mind. Each of the wagons had stoves if

Secret Death Defying Escape Finally Told

they needed heat at night; all seemed to have plenty of beer, or whatever they needed. The Russians had given them food and supplies for the trip. They had received instructions to stop at pre-determined places along the route to resupply as needed. We didn't tell the Russians of the supplies that had come from the store.

In addition to all of this, we had a plow, a seeder, a small disc, and a three-piece drag — a complete combination for planting a small field. Of course, we planned to reopen a store in the new land but, in the meantime, we would stake out as much of the land as we could and work it. The Russians promised many things, but a lot of travelers had stopped at the store during their journeys, and those who had been through said there hadn't been much preparation for newcomers to Russia. So we had to use our own for awhile.

Max and Albert told all who accompanied them to take seeds and food, canning jars, animals, etc. They urged them to be prepared, but most didn't have much to take along. That is, of course, one reason they had closed their own store's doors so abruptly. Many people owed the store money and wanted to charge more. Collecting was impossible, so there was no use continuing. They decided to bite the bullet and move on.

It took several weeks of steady traveling, although they did not press the horses too hard. This was early spring, and they were determined to arrive in plenty of time to get some breaking and planting done yet this spring. All of the people in our wagon train were from our village, but we expected to see more immigrants as we traveled.

Each time we stopped at a village where we were supposed to receive supplies and food, we were cut short. There was a limit; if we really wanted more, they could find more — for a price. Max knew a lot of people with influence, and he threatened to contact these people if we didn't receive our share. Just before we were about to leave, they would remember where more supplies were and we would receive our allotment. Real strange how that worked.

We finally arrived at the so-called land office, and we were told we were early. We weren't expected yet! What were we to do?

Max blew his stack, even though he expected all along that this would happen. He accused them of breaking their promise, and announced we would be going back. They got a little excited then and told us where our land was located.

One of our people was a well wisher, and a good one. A well wisher is a man who can hold a willow branch or another branch in a certain way, and when he went over a water vein, there would be a pull on it. That's where you dig your well! We immediately employed him to find water, so we knew where to build.

After a lot of shouting and haggling, we got a tract of land that looked good. Some of those who followed didn't fare as well. We were the first to arrive, plus they felt they better let us get started. The well wisher found water in many places, so the legal papers were drawn up.

Secret Death Defying Escape Finally Told

Digging a well by hand. Note the steps cut in the sides to get up and down. As they filled the buckets, the men on top pulled them up.

Opportunities Of A New Land

In a week, the stakes were in and each family began planning, but there was no lumber! So they began digging wells. The water was about 30 feet down. The wells, of course, were dug with spades, and the holes were four to five feet across! Some cut a little of the spade handle off, so they could maneuver them more easily. When they got down where it was too deep to take the dirt out of the hole, they filled a bucket attached to a rope, and the men on top of the ground would pull it up, dump it, and send it back down. They took turns in the hole. When they got near the water, they put a rope around the man in the hole in case he punched through to the water. Sometimes, the stream of water would fill the hole real fast — too fast to get out!

As they went down, they cut steps in the side of the hole to climb up and down as they worked. The walls seemed to be of clay until you got near the water. There it was sand. They tried to get as much of the sand out as possible, or the pump would plug and the well would not flow well.

The families helped each other, digging one well at a time. It would take about five days of good digging to get the well flowing. They had to build a well cover immediately, so children and animals did not fall into the hole.

Because many of these people owed Max and Albert money, they were happy to work off their bills so they could qualify for credit in the future. A well was dug for each house and for the site where they wanted the store. Then they went right to work in the fields and got some planting done. Since the Russians hadn't provided plows or any equipment, Max and Albert loaned theirs out so each fami-

Secret Death Defying Escape Finally Told

ly could have a garden spot. They also advanced seed for their gardens. About four weeks passed and still no Russians, no lumber, seed, money, or supplies.

Max and Albert were both above average build, and they feared no man. So one bright morning, they rode about five miles to the government office and demanded to know where their materials were. Max and Albert gave them the worst slapping around they'd ever had, though not with fists, just threats and shoves.

In a few days enough lumber for one good-sized building arrived, and about half as much seed as they needed. Thus ensued another shouting match! This time, the top government official was there, and he said that if the colonists gave them anymore trouble, they would receive nothing!

They wrote to their friends in government in Germany and asked for help. Because of the slow communication, even if they did receive assistance from them, it would likely not be in time to build houses before the horrible winter set in. They decided to build sod houses. Everyone was tired of the wagon houses by now. Besides, they would freeze to death in them quickly during the winter.

It was decided to build a store with the lumber. All pitched in to build it and kept track of their time. Everything went well, and it was built in two days. It had a good well with a pump and a floor. Behind it, they put up a sod building that butted tight against the north side. All of this was needed for storage, because they had brought much with them. At first they hid most of the supplies in

Opportunities Of A New Land

the sod house. It was closed off and couldn't be seen from the store side.

A sod house is built by cutting strips of sod with a plow and horses, and then placed one on top of the other. It's best if a framework is made to gird the walls until they can be watered and start rooting in. If it's built too late in the fall so it can't grow much, it must be girded with a framework or it will slide out.

There was a river beside us, so getting small trees for a framework was not a problem. Each home had a frame, generally on the south side so they could build a door and a window or two for light. It was decided that all would work together to plow, cut and haul trees, and build frameworks

Working their fields with oxen.

Secret Death Defying Escape Finally Told

Sod houses were built first and then as they got lumber, they added on.

so two to three houses could be built simultaneously. Names were drawn out of a hat to determine whose house would be next. Houses were built so when the lumber came, they could add to the south side and continue to live in it.

When the houses were half through one day, we looked up and saw wagons! Lumber, food, supplies, seed! Something had happened! It was all carefully unloaded and when the lumber was counted, there was enough for about half of the houses. There were 30 families here, so names were drawn again for the lumber.

Decision time. We weren't sure how much could be built by fall, and if the sod houses weren't built while they could still grow, they wouldn't be much good. It was decided to finished the sod huts first. Then, if more lumber hadn't arrived by that time, we would use half a house of lumber for each one. That way, each family would have the same sod and one large wood room.

The horses, cattle, goats, sheep and chickens also needed shelter. A corral was built immediately for the animals, and a fenced pasture was built for grazing during the day. The goats had to be in the houses, along with any small calves they had. Otherwise, wolves and mountain lions would have them in an instant.

The colonists worked feverishly until fall, gardening, harvesting, building, and cutting wood for winter. The Russians could not believe it! They said that other settlements in the area had one or two families living together and a shelter for the animals. That's all most had done. None had crops in, and only a few had gardens.

The Russians were fairly regular with supplies, food and everyone was happy. The summer was quite hot, so our crops were nothing special. New ground requires more water, so the crops produced were slim, but we had lots for feed. We cut hay in the low spots, so we were ready for the winter. The women and children did many of the chores and the work that was done. They did the haying and gardening. The chairs we had were tree stumps cut in the woods. The women and children hauled them to our settlement, painted them and put them in the homes. All of the furniture was made there.

Max and Albert had their houses connected to the store, so they could go back and forth without going outside. The main farm where the animals were housed was connected to a half dozen houses. They were built against the barn so in the winter, they could feed and water without going outside. This would be especially important when it was storming.

Secret Death Defying Escape Finally Told

Max's and Albert's residences were built onto the store.

All of the wells were covered either by their houses or a shed. Most of the people did not have pumps. They used a pail on a rope, dropped it down, and pulled up the water.

The people worked together and were happy. Though it had been snowing for about two weeks, the weather was not stormy. The hunting was good; deer were plentiful. The men organized a hunt, surrounded a large area, and moved in. They shot enough venison for a year. It was cold enough to store it outside, but it had to be kept in an outside shed or a box that animals couldn't get into. These were frugal people. They worked together to butcher the deer, cut them up, and divided them equally so all would have enough. They made home sausage by the wagon load! The hides were cured and used to make gloves, caps and slippers. They began canning their meat. This was the only way they had to preserve it.

Opportunities Of A New Land

One day a fancy buggy came up the driveway with a couple of well-dressed men. They asked if we were happy. Other than the fact that we were all supposed to be getting checks and were behind on supplies, we were okay. They could not believe the progress! They had with them two young artists, and they asked if they could draw pictures and write down the progress — take their pictures to the queen. We agreed. The government official had cash for everyone with him, so now everyone was happy!

A still was always running plus homemade beer. Different ingredients were added to the alcohol, and the favorite was kimmel. They also mixed hot water, sugar and burnt sugar to the alcohol. A small drink was enough to give a real wallop! I can't say I ever saw anyone drunk, but sometimes they talked a lot. The Russians also enjoyed the drinks.

One of the reasons this group got a head start was because Max and Albert brought along their saws. We got a year's head start, plus they always kept things moving.

Max and Albert's mother, Louise, was in the store working every day. She was in her fifties, but really didn't look or act it. Her husband, Ed Wolske, was killed when Albert was just two years old. She and Ed had worked to get their store in good shape for five years before they had any children. The store had belonged to Ed's dad, but they really improved it! Ed was Jewish, which wasn't very popular in those days. I doubt many knew he was. He was a big man and had rather hard features. He had dark hair, a wrinkled forehead, and knurled hands. He worked 18 hours a day,

Secret Death Defying Escape Finally Told

and was a real businessman. He developed the only feed mill, where they converted wheat to flour and cereal. He had thousands of dollars in credit on the books at all times. He charged a little more in the store and the mill made money, so he was doing very well.

Max and Albert were raised in the store. When Ed was kicked in the head by his stallion and killed, Louise closed the store until the funeral was over and then took over. The employees they had continued working for Louise. Ed and Louise were the best loved people in the village. The townspeople didn't care that Ed was Jewish. Louise was a local girl whose father was a German farmer. Ed and Louise had helped almost everyone at one time or another with credit. As a rule, they were repaid and got along great. There was no bank in the village, so they also acted like a bank exchange much of the time.

Several nurses and midwives lived in the village to handle minor health concerns, including the delivery of children. But, although Max had been making a lot of offers, he had been unable to attract a doctor. Max and Albert brought a wide variety of over-the-counter medications with them; the people had been healthy. The most common cures were home cures.

As an example, the villagers used to take onions in the fall and put them in a press. The juice didn't even taste like onion; it was sweet and good! This was given to children one teaspoon each day to keep them healthy. I remember taking this onion juice as a small child, like yesterday! The menu was passed down over 200 years. Onions and garlic were

Opportunities Of A New Land

important in the German diet.

Vegetables have always been an important part of their meals. Cabbage was popular. I think Germans like to eat!

Obviously, the mortality rate was not as it is today. Baby deaths and elderly deaths were many times what they are today. Appendicitis, or ruptured appendix, was deadly in most all instances, even as late as the 1930s. Until penicillin was invented, it meant almost certain death. Parasites set in and poisoned the system, and there was no cure. Blood poison, childbirth, and many other health fears existed that we don't even think about today. These were hardy people. Those who lived through it were really hardy!

Plain sod house. The same here as well as in the Ukraine.

Secret Death Defying Escape Finally Told

CHAPTER 2

A Brutal Winter- The Warmth Of Friendship

ANOTHER DAY DAWNED and here came a train of wagons. Finally the rest of our lumber, just in time for winter! The villagers were glad they had put one room on each sod house; at least everyone had quarters. Some people had no children left and there were unmarried people, including widows and bachelors, who didn't need more room, so Albert and Max figured out a fair price and bought their lumber. The lumber was separated and on the first warm winter day, everyone pitched in. A new building was built to house the flour mill. In a day, they framed it in so they could work inside when it got cold.

This was the village's first elevator. It had a leg to pull the grain up in so-called cups. It was powered by horses walking in a circle and pulling the grain up on a lift. It was then directed to whatever bin they wanted. Now they could handle different kinds of grain at the same time.

Red durum was common then. I don't know if it's related to today's durum which is used for making pasta. It had deep colored (brown red) kernels not any larger than spring wheat. It had a partial hull on it. A brush device was developed to brush off the hulls and let the kernels fall through the mill or sieves. Speltz was used for milling. It was the forerunner to our hard wheat. It also had loose hulls.

Secret Death Defying Escape Finally Told

Horses pulling the grist wheels to grind the flour at the mill. They were blindfolded and went around in a circle, pulling the wheels.

Peddlers visited the village offering the store a variety of items. The larger the quantity they bought, the better the price. Part of the new building was to be for storage. They paid the people for their surplus lumber and began pounding nails. When it was enclosed, they continued to work inside. They built fires to keep warm, and had a hot pot of tea, cookies, and maybe a sandwich at break time. Albert supervised that project. The people were happy to be earning money for themselves, since they were paid by Max and Albert.

They voted to name the store, the mill, and everything our one name, "Wolske!"

A Brutal Winter – The Warmth Of Friendship

Even though bad weather was potential, the signs indicated it would be a mild winter. Max and a couple other men chose four of the biggest, strongest horses and left for the fatherland to try to personally get a doctor. Several young men from our area were in medical school. Hopefully, we could talk them into coming to the new land! We loaded food and lots of warm clothing, even bed rolls. We were fortunate to find a warm bed each night. The trail was good, so we made good time. The horses had plenty of oats, and we put them up at night in livery farms. There were many more travelers than we expected.

It took a lot less time traveling home than going east with the wagons. We had a nice reunion, and when we told our friends how it was going they all wanted to come. The

Animals had to be kept in corrals at night.

Secret Death Defying Escape Finally Told

med students said they had some offers, but hadn't made up their minds. We told them where we were.

We also got a promise from two young doctors, but they couldn't come until spring. We told them we would have a new house waiting for them.

Max then went to different suppliers and ordered furniture and other articles for his store. We headed back after five days and couldn't believe the nice weather we were having. Max bought geese and ducks that we put in a thin sack on the house. They froze quickly and stayed frozen. He bought some other special foods that we hadn't had — lots of candy for one thing. In fact, about 100 pounds of bulk candy to sell at the store.

Max felt thankful for what we had done. He wanted to put on a special meal for everyone in the village. Ours was a Lutheran group; the Catholics were in a village farther south. One of the men in the colony studied Martin Luther's writings and was a certified clergyman. Each Sunday, we had services at the store but this would be too small soon. The families had more children, and the children were getting bigger! Maybe we could have a town hall and a church, all in one.

When Max saw how much poverty his friends lived with in Germany, he wept. He was a big man, but soft hearted. He stopped the horses after we had ridden out an hour or so, and asked the others to bow their heads in prayer. He prayed aloud for those who had less than we and thanked God for what we had. No one had ever seen him do this, but he had been so moved.

A Brutal Winter – The Warmth Of Friendship

We had left the extra horse we took with us for the doctor, with one of the groups who promised he would come. He really appreciated it. He had been walking everywhere and would enjoy the ride.

As we journeyed back to our new colony, we took all of our merchandise into the hotels at night or it would have been stolen. Quite a chore! The wind was on our back going home, but it was still cool.

We were glad to have been back home in Germany, and felt our visit had been productive. We had to take lumber from the pile (somebody's house) and start building for the doctor. We had to hope and pray for a nice week so we could get it started.

Albert and the boys had made real progress when we were gone. The storeroom was finished. In fact, it had some supplies in it, and the mill was nearly done.

It was now the Christmas season, and the freezing weather just wouldn't let up — 20 to 30 degrees below with so many snowstorms! People from other colonies were stopping at the store. They found the Wolske's had so much to choose from. They couldn't believe it! If they didn't have money, no credit was granted. The store, of course, did a lot of business from the 30 families living in the colony.

One day a fancy sleigh with six well dressed men came in and asked questions about where our property line was. Max moved the line about 30 rods over. They were planning for more people. Max informed them, "Before you move anyone else in here, you enlarge it for us. We have teenagers growing up every year, people getting married, and we need

Secret Death Defying Escape Finally Told

more room now." He and Albert reminded them that nobody would be here if we hadn't developed it. "Okay, okay," was the reply. We received a whole new addition of good land. After the papers were signed, Max and Albert took them to the back of the store and gave them schnapps and fed them.

This was an especially happy Christmas! The geese and ducks were a surprise, as were family gifts for each family and all the children. Max had ordered them when he was back in Germany.

Finally, the weather turned. We had a few nice days, and everybody grabbed their hammers to start the doctor's house. Three days was all this crew needed to get it framed in and boarded shut and windows in.

It had been snowing hard for three days. The sky in the west was dark blue and looked bad. When this storm hit during the night, it was like a bull hitting the side of the house! It lasted four days and was so cold we were glad our beds were in the sod part of the house. The insulation in the house didn't do the job; the house part was cold. We decided to make some changes next summer! Now we were glad the lumber didn't come early. It's a good thing we had put up sod houses.

We were barely poking our noses out after the storm when a sled came up. It was from another colony, a small one that came in last summer and didn't make much progress. They were out of fuel and low on food. They wanted to know if their children could stay a few days until they could cut some trees. We asked, "How many kids? and is the fire out?" No but it will be shortly! Max gave them three days supply and we put it in their sleigh. No use letting their houses cool down. We told them to take the fuel home, come back and cut trees for a few days. Then they'd have wood for all winter. They returned, and when everyone came in the house and we offered the children food, we could tell they were really hungry. This was partly their own fault; they shouldn't have believed Russian promises!

The little children said that cooked wheat was all they had. We also prepared cooked wheat, taking wheat from the bin, washing it, soaking it and cooking it. Wonderful cereal, but three times a day all week! Kids don't like that!

We asked why they hadn't at least shot deer. They had no guns! We asked if they had money. Yes, a little. Max offered to sell them two guns for fifty dollars. (For clarity, money amounts are referred to in "dollars.") That is what they cost him. He even included shells. He told them, "Now when you are by the river cutting trees, be on the lookout for deer, so you can have meat. Our groups are down there trapping mink, fox and other animals. They say there are deer there every day."

They arranged to meet there in the morning and shot some deer. Within 30 minutes, they had bagged a half dozen deer. Since they had only six families, there would be plenty of meat until we could get more. We also gave them bread, sausage, onions, and carrots. They were very grateful.

They had built two buildings, sod huts large enough to house three families. Two walls inside ran all the way through. Not a bad idea if you all get along well, but that

Secret Death Defying Escape Finally Told

The first church they built, soon after settling.

doesn't always happen. They were warmer and stronger. The lack of honesty by the Russians had caused this colony's problems. They were not as experienced a group, nor did they have a leader like Albert and Max. It's going to be a long time until spring for them.

Before the day was over, another group came to the store with the same problem — no food. They had five families in one building, and had been waiting to no avail for the Russians to come with their winter rations. They had little flour left, and bread is all they had had in nearly three weeks. They also had the same problem with hunting — no guns.

They had some money, so Max gave them the same deal as the first group. We all went out the next morning and shot four deer for them. The last we saw they were going to make sausage, steak, roast, everything. God bless.

A Brutal Winter – The Warmth Of Friendship

By Christmas, the city hall was finished enough to use. A large stove was installed and the Christmas party was to be held there. Unbeknownst to the pastor, the villagers' plan was to present it as a church and just use a side room for meeting. They asked the pastor to have the Christmas program there. They went to the river, and brought back a large evergreen tree, fashioned a wooden cross from tree boughs, and made pews from boards and tree stumps. Al and Max received many heartfelt handmade doilies and crafts with embroideries. The show of appreciation for one another was vibrant. About that time, Max asked if everyone would bow their heads while he led in prayer. Not only did he give thanks from the heart, but prayed for those who were less fortunate. Then they announced to the pastor that this was his church from now on. He was overwhelmed. He gave a brief sermon, gave thanks, and could barely stop crying for joy.

Max giving thanks to the Lord for all of their blessings on this first Christmas.

Secret Death Defying Escape Finally Told

Their first Christmas in the new land.

The next day we feasted on geese, ducks, chicken, beef, venison and all the fixings, German style cabbage, homemade pies, and on and on. Max, however, could hardly finish his meal. He was so bothered that the two colonies within a few miles each way from us had nothing until we helped them get the guns and deer. He suggested, "Now that we have all eaten and there is much left over, let's take a box of food to them! Wouldn't that make us all feel good!" All agreed!

The ladies carefully packed a large box for each. Then a box with candy and gifts was packed. Some of the children wanted to share even what they had received. A sleigh full of people went to each place to wish them a merry Christmas, to have a toast and a prayer with them, and give them their boxes. This was truly real joy. First from us as we prepared the boxes, and then from them after they received it. It was a Christmas we'll always remember. (Besides that, we had leftovers for three days!)

Another storm was upon us. Winter here does not let up. They tell us this is a bad one.

CHAPTER **3**

Establishing Themselves In The New Land

WE ALL GOT THROUGH the winter and, by spring, the two little colonies purchased seed and supplies from the store and used up their money. The Russians had promised a plow and drill, but provided nothing.

Our village made them a deal. We would put the crop in if they would work it off. We had buildings to build, and they could be paid for by working. They agreed.

People were bringing wheat from quite a distance now to the mill, and we were selling flour and cereal almost as fast as we could fill the 25, 50 and 100 pound bags. We had been very low on wheat, so we encouraged not only our colony but others to plant wheat. We promised to pay top price, and offer supplies in trade too.

We, too, had a lot of extra land to break this year. It was as busy as a beehive here, when we saw the longest wagon train ever, pulling in. What was this? They stopped by the store, and as we looked out, it must have been a half mile long. We went out and they were talking German. They had left the father's land!

Max asked, "Where are you headed?" "Right here," was their reply. "Where are the Russians? Who's in charge?" Nobody. The Russians hadn't shown up yet. They had signed these poor devils up, and given them wagons and horses to come here!

Secret Death Defying Escape Finally Told

Germans heading for the Ukraine in search of a better life.

We asked how they knew where to come? They brought out the artists' drawings that were made here last summer. They showed them a bit of heaven! They had supplies with them for a week or two, but where is their land? We felt lucky we had signed on the extra land last fall. The men took them to the end of our territory, and said their land must be beyond here. They made camp there. We marked the line where our land ended, and the men continued putting up fence around it.

The newcomers had some money and came every day to buy supplies. They really went after candy, tobacco, flour, cereal, and sugar, things they hadn't brought with them.

To my surprise, in about two to four days, the Russians showed up! They didn't bring supplies though. How are they going to build and plan? They had one wagon with bags of wheat seed, but no way to plant it. They gave them all money and told them to buy from Wolskes what they needed.

Max and Albert were now feeling increasingly strained. We had only three plows and seeders, and with the extra land we couldn't plant theirs until our own was done. We told them how much money we needed, and they agreed.

First, we broke and worked their garden plots and then the wheat fields. They did not have nearly enough garden seed, but we sold them what we had. We sold them wire and posts to make fence for them as well. Then we showed them where and how to dig wells. We suggested that they build sod houses like ours. Don't believe the Russians! The Russian agents were shorting all these people and were selling the extras in the black market.

The newcomers went through the process to get supplies, but they received less than we had, and they didn't have leaders like Max and Albert Wolske. We gave them all the help we could. They didn't always listen very well. They couldn't believe the Russians weren't coming through.

By fall, they had received lumber for about a dozen houses for all their people. By this time, they realized they better dig or die. They didn't get very good sod houses, because they waited until the growing season was over. They did take our advice to use the lumber they received to put a small room on each sod house. This would make it more livable.

One fall day, four or five riders came riding in quickly from the northwest. They were our neighbors from the

Secret Death Defying Escape Finally Told

Bandits wiping out a small group of settlers.

small colony of six families. What's up? They had been raided! Rough looking people had come in, started to take what they wanted, food, and demanded more. They loaded these supplies into a wagon. Then they grabbed two young girls. That's when the men went back to the bedroom, grabbed some guns, and shot these two guys. They also shot at the others, but they hit their horses and got away. They asked us, what could they do?

We took a dozen guys on horseback and went to the village. We discovered they had been watching the riders and, when they came for help, the bandits went back in force. They raped the women, shot four men who tried to stop them, and took another load of supplies.

I told them they couldn't stay there. They were too small to fight. Everything they had was loaded up and brought to

Establishing Themselves In The New Land

our colony. We had built several extra houses in the summer for future use for ourselves, but now they would be theirs. In fact, we traded their land for the houses and gave them jobs in the mill or wherever they were needed. They were happy!

As time passed, the bandits got rougher. Max ordered more guns. He didn't receive them, so he went to Germany and got a load himself with lots of ammunition. Any of the colonists who were willing to fight and learned to shoot could buy a gun. Max got well paid for this trip.

Some of the other settlers bought guns, but decided to go back. They were afraid. Max and Albert bought their land for a small price and whatever else they wished to sell. They were satisfied, because they were returning with much

Colonists being surprised by bandits. Many died in these attacks.

Secret Death Defying Escape Finally Told

more money than they came with. The colonists now had a lot of land to farm, but acquired two more plows so they could get it done. Several of the families who wanted to stay came and moved in. We were now quite a village.

The store had to be doubled in size and the peddlers were here nearly every day unloading. They liked to come here because we could take the whole load, and they didn't have to unload here and there. Albert and about ten other people worked in the warehouses and the store. They also added a butchering plant and sold meat. The meat was mostly cured, as there was no way to keep it from spoiling. They butchered two days a week, so if townspeople wanted a fresh roast or another cut, they could go on those days. So a lot of fresh meat was sold too. Sheep and goats were also in demand. They paid well for livestock, so everyone raised them. Cured meat, of course, always was a big seller.

Today is a sad day. We were informed that the people who left to go back to Germany were attacked and killed. The bandits, who lived in the forest not too far away, took everything. There is no army or police force to keep order.

The relatives of the family who had decided to stay with us went with another group of men to retrieve the bodies. They found that four of the women were missing. The bandits must have taken them. The family wanted us to go after them, but that would be suicide. They are hidden; they see you coming, and you don't have a chance.

Max and Albert put up a firing range and showed everyone how to be effective marksmen. A number of the men had served in the German army and they set up the defense

Establishing Themselves In The New Land

tactics. A stockade was built all around and Max and another man trained a large group to use it. We could close our gates and we would be one large fighting force. One of the men was an expert with dogs. He trained them to kill, and we felt pretty safe. The three military men were responsible for defense.

There was great anguish over the four women who were captured. Two of the girls who had decided to stay and were now living with us, were daughters of two women. The situation was a difficult one. Though the missing women were not well known to us, they were wonderful people. But could we risk the lives of fathers and brothers in a shootout? As long as those bandits are there, they would always be a threat. They prefer raiding travelers along the trail, as most travelers have no guns and are a small, unprotected band. If we left our colony, not only would they attack our suppliers and customers, they would attack us too. But it would be on our conscience if we did nothing.

It was important to figure out a way to rescue the women with no loss of life. We decided to turn it over to the military.

They decided to take about four wagons with old horses, and possibly tie a horse behind, so we looked like peasants. On the side the bandits would attack from, we could place logs or heavy timbers four feet high. So if they shot at us, the bullets wouldn't penetrate. The wagons would be filled with shooters who would duck down and hide.

As the bandits rode toward us and got close enough, we could easily shoot them from the lead wagon. The lead dri-

Secret Death Defying Escape Finally Told

ver would signal and all would rise, aim, and fire. The wagons would all stop so we could shoot better. As soon as the first wagon fired, the second would jump up, shoot, and then the next would follow in quick succession. By this time, the lead wagon should be reloaded if there were any remaining to shoot. The element of complete surprise and the fact that we had a standing shot should be in our favor. We should be very safe. Also our men had been practicing, and were good shots.

While the shooting was taking place, a dozen riders would sneak into the trees from the south. They would ride until they found signs of their hideout and lay back in hiding. When the bandits took off toward the wagons, these riders were supposed to sneak through the trees, ride as close as they dared, dismount, and move up on foot. Here, surprise was the main asset we would have. This group had pistols, which are quicker in close combat.

With our plan in place, we headed out. As expected, the bandits closed in fast and looked to be about 30 to 60 men. Just as planned, the first, then second, then third wagon fired. One man was getting away! He's hard to hit. Shoot the horse. Now he's running and the rifles began at once. He dropped. Another was wounded, but now it's all over. We took the guns and ammunition quickly, rounded up the horses, put riders on them, and headed for their camp.

The bandits were watching the goings-on from their hideout and when they saw what had happened, they ran for their horses to make their escape. By now, our men in the trees had arrived and, as they came riding out of the

Establishing Themselves In The New Land

barn to leave, they were gunned down. Not one bandit was left.

The women were alive and other than the unwanted treatment they received, they were okay. The leaders had decided to take these women as their mates, and did not allow handling by any of the others. In fact, several had objected and lost their lives. This was a big break for the women. At least they only had one each to satisfy.

Some may think this is not the behavior of a pious Christian people. We had no way to handle or to keep them; they made their living by murdering. Our action was self defense and rescue. We prayed for forgiveness and gave them a proper burial. We had cleaned out this group, but there were many more down the line.

We took everything of value. They had lots of boots, guns, money, food, sleighs, saddles, etc. We loaded it all, including a stove, horse feed, etc., and took it home. This was all stolen property. When we were through, we torched the hiding place so it wouldn't be a place for another group to move into.

After this, we realized that we needed a bank building where we could store money and valuables. This group of thieves had an unbelievable amount of gold, silver and cash. This, we felt, belonged to all the villagers, but where would we put it?

The people who had come in to the south of us had a few people who knew how to make bricks. We had the right kind of clay, and we had a good machine shop. So they made a machine to make bricks and the first brick building

Secret Death Defying Escape Finally Told

was our bank. It was thick walled and quite fireproof. All the villagers worked together on this. One of Albert's sons had returned to Germany four years earlier to learn finance, bookkeeping, and banking. He was to run the bank.

In the spring, both our doctors arrived, and we clamored to build a four-bed hospital. Medical supplies came in slowly, but we were fortunate that no major illness occurred other than some deaths that were incurable in those days. We had gotten by.

We had a pretty good school going now, but we had totally outgrown it. So with the advent of bricks came a new school, clinic, hospital, pharmacy, and dental office. We, of course, were drawing business from the other colonies who didn't have these services. We even had many Russian officers and agents coming through our offices. These were not common facilities in Russia.

Along with financial prosperity through a rapidly growing population, oftentimes come social and moral problems. On the domestic front and in private lives, there was some hanky-panky — experimenting by the young and crossing over by some adults. Unlike today, if a girl became pregnant, there was a lot of pressure on the father to get married. Unwed mothers were few. Marriage was considered sacred, and divorce didn't occur. By living in this tight social structure, laws were naturally set. If a man beat up his wife, "bruisers" would be over to beat him up. They had their own justice.

One very serious problem looming its head was intermarriage. Forty to fifty families lived in the colonies, and

Establishing Themselves In The New Land

most families had many children. The new colony had perhaps 150 families, so after 20 years there were many requests for cousins to marry cousins. A morals standard was set up with a board of directors sworn to secrecy. The pastor, doctor, Albert's son Jake from the bank, and Max and Albert formed this board. They determined that second cousins could marry, though first cousins could not. The colonists were advised of the standards for marriage.

In 1796 Queen Catherine died. The colonists wondered how this would affect their future. How would the czar treat them now? The Germans had been lied to, cheated on…the Russians could not be trusted. The death of Queen Catherine was a fearful event for the Germans.

The sister colony adjacent to us had to build their main quarters according to the Russians' guidelines. They were built with eight apartments on a single level with a basement. They were attached to one another via an enclosed walkway. In fact, all the buildings and barns were connected. They did allow them to keep their original houses of sod with a small wooden room.

As they finished building, people moved from the sod houses to the buildings. The houses were never totally unoccupied because materials came in slowly, marriages continually took place, and more colonists came from the homeland. They moved into the original houses. The new colony never had a store, bank, or school, and never really was able to have the products and services our colony had, because they didn't have much capital to buy what they needed.

Our men and I guess theirs, too, had a big fur business, since our settlements were located on the river. We had rich

Secret Death Defying Escape Finally Told

hunting and trapping grounds. The fur buyers came almost every month during the winter, but the Russians were chiselers, paying only a portion of what the furs were worth. So

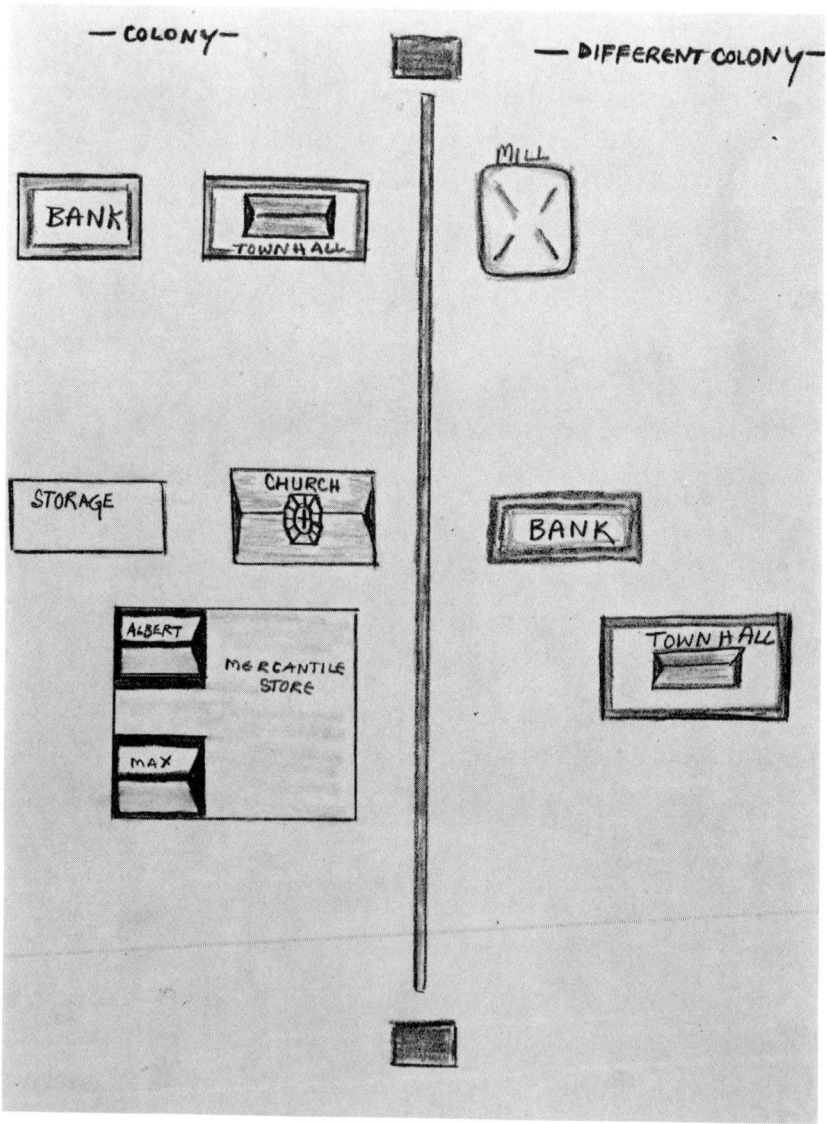

Establishing Themselves In The New Land

we collected the furs, and stretched and readied them for market. There would always be some inferior furs — some that were torn, animals that didn't mature…We decided that these were the only ones the Russians would get. Ninety percent were good and valuable. They were secretly stashed away, and when the weather broke they were carefully boxed and loaded. The furs were worth many thousands of dollars each year. They were loaded into good wagons with tops to keep them dry. An additional six wagons were loaded with shooters to protect them from bandits littering the roads.

Of course, we did not want to be caught by the Russians, so we took side roads and they were more dangerous. It was common to be attacked twice in one trip. The bandits were desperate people and the lowest creatures in the world. The wagons were reinforced with double walls and heavy planks on the inside. A bullet would not penetrate. Many bullets riddled the outer walls, but the second wall remained strong. Our wagon riders never lost a skirmish, but we gained a lot of rifles, horses and saddles.

We were not supposed to be trading with Germany, but the prices were ten times better than if we had sold to Russia. We had agreed to deposit the money into a savings account with a strong German bank. We had to use the name of a German citizen we could trust.

One of Max's and Albert's cousins was a Lutheran pastor. He agreed to put it in his name, and Max had his name on the account. They paid the pastor $500 per year to do this, and he was happy. This year we sold more than $10,000

Secret Death Defying Escape Finally Told

worth, which by today's standards would probably be $100,000. This was a business of the settlement and the money belonged to all of us.

The trappers had their own quarters and didn't do any other work. Much of their work was done at night when the moon was out. They napped when they were tired, and skinned all day long. The trappers also became specialized, some skinning, some stretching and some trapping. The arrangement worked great.

The Russians came by in the spring and asked where their furs were stored. We always gave them excuses. Bad year ...

For 10 years, we had a hey-day with our fur industry. More than $100,000 in German banks at 12% interest.

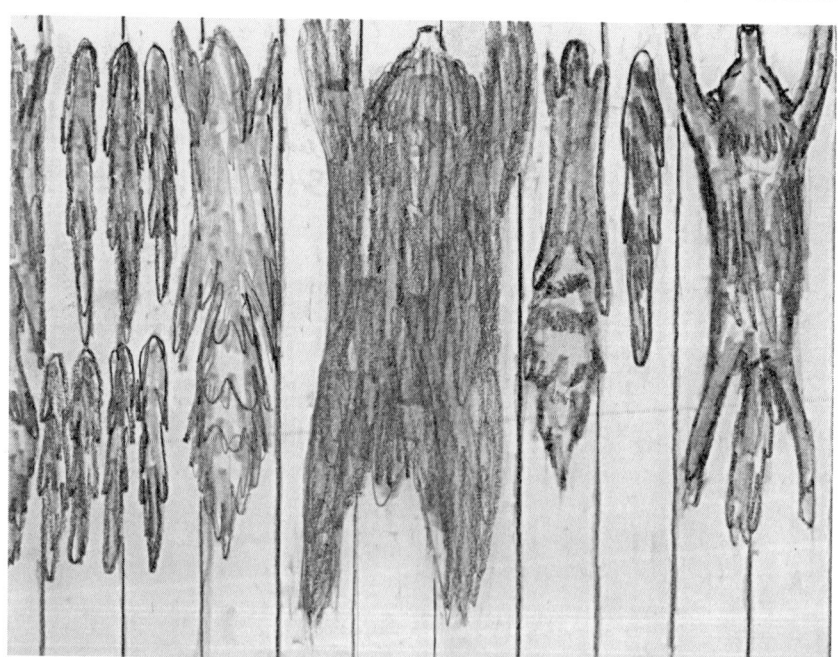

Trapping and hunting was an important part of colonial life.

Establishing Themselves In The New Land

This was kept very secret. The colonists had a lot of personal money in Germany too. Albert and Max's stores were doing well financially, and they too were storing money in Germany. They had always been leaders in building the community and improving the standard of living for the settlement. At least 25 youth were in high school and college in Kiev, a neighboring city. The people had more goods and services than either Russia or Germany. But now it came to a screeching halt. The edict dropped on all of them.

Max and Albert had always been careful about not making their Jewish background prominent, even though the older folks knew their father was Jewish. They were never criticized; they had always been revered. They had never known their father, but seemed to have his ambitions and goals, and their mother had taken a strong hold of the store for perhaps 10 years after his death. It was almost as though he were still here. This was never mentioned to the Russians, and Max and Albert's children returned to Germany for schooling, because they were somehow afraid of being identified as Jewish in the Russian schools.

Secret Death Defying Escape Finally Told

CHAPTER 4

Changing Times, Unrest, Taxes

THEY WERE GIVEN a 20-year exemption from paying taxes when they settled in Russia. This time had expired several years ago, but Max had talked them into waiting a few years because of the money he had lost in initially establishing his business. The agents who normally came also liked it here. When the day was over, they would have a feast with all the trimmings and a dance. They would go home with gifts they didn't have in Russia. So the men generally got their way! Culture and music had an important purpose, and we had quite a number of good musicians — violins, accordions, and pianos were the most popular.

But now the edict had come down! Tax 10% on everything! For three of four weeks, every article, each pound of flour, cereal and all had to be counted and 10% paid. Every cow, hog, lamb, and chicken sold by a farmer had to be accounted for and the farmer paid a 10% tax. The bank, clinic, pharmacy were taxed...no store was left exempt.

No guns! They wanted all our guns. The men had anticipated this for some time, so they didn't have more than 10% of their stock in visible storage. The rest were hidden!

The same pertained to money and pharmacy goods.

It was obvious we would need to play a different ballgame. This was like paying 10% more with less income. It

Secret Death Defying Escape Finally Told

was a bad omen and everyone knew it. It may be the beginning of other problems.

The country was always in some kind of war, and the last thing we wanted was to have our boys in the Russian army. We thought they might leave the ones alone who were at home on the farm, especially if they're married. The boys in school in Kiev were too handy. At the end of this quarter, we decided to get them home.

The clan immediately had a meeting and made some decisions. By now there were nearly 200 families. Max's son, Christian, was in college in Germany studying law. His daughter, Amelia, was also there studying to be a teacher. They also studied languages. This skill was needed in those days, with many travelers and people moving around.

Christian was planning to get married in the spring to a girl he had met in college. Max contacted him to make arrangements to move the students from Kiev to a German college. He didn't trust the Russians, and Germany offered a better education.

It is now 1825. Russia has thousands of Germans occupying land from the Black Sea to Siberia. Their country was expanding and its people were faring quite well. The colonies felt the kick when the taxation started, but they were much better off than in Germany. Most opted to stay in Russia, though now America had become a dream. Many put their money together and traveled to America. The homestead act was on and they could get free land. All they had to do was claim it.

Changing Times, Unrest, Taxes

Their neighboring country, Norway was overcrowded, and they had exported thousands to the upper Midwest. Norwegians were settling in the Dakotas, Minnesota, Michigan, Wisconsin, and Canada or New York.

The Germans in Russia would have to break away from Russia after already leaving Germany, and then cross the sea to America. Some Germans in Germany, however, traveled straight to America. For most though, they did not have enough money.

The Jewish community in Max and Albert's hometown in Germany had wanted so badly to go to Russia as we had, but they were even more distrustful of the Russians than the Germans were! Now, though, Germany was looking less and less desirable, so they decided to move. Albert knew many

The heat and the smoke from the furnace went all along the wall. They made their beds on this three-foot ledge to keep warm. Oldest ones were farthest from the furnace.

45

Secret Death Defying Escape Finally Told

of them, as they lived in the Jewish section of the city when they were children. He had kept up his acquaintanceship each time they returned to visit, several times a year. He kept them informed of how we were doing and offered to take a half a dozen families now. In three months, we could handle a few more.

The men kept building; they always had an order to the government for additional lumber. There were always a couple homes unoccupied.

Most of the settlers had already taken German names. This was the safest way to go and, of course, many Jews and Germans were intermarried. We received the message that they would be at the border on a certain day.

Traveling is trickier now. No one is supposed to have guns except the army, so we had to have them well concealed. We built a false bottom in the wagon and stored them there. We took our battle wagons with the double walls. Bandits were thicker than ever now. They knew that most travelers were defenseless.

We met our friends at the border and headed for home. As we were talking about the dangers, the bandits came riding out of the forest to the clearing. We would surprise them. We told the newcomers to get down out of sight in their wagons. When they came within range, we executed our usual plan and they fell like flies. There were about a dozen bandits in this group. We saw seven fall, and the rest retreated. We ran out and took their guns, which are really valuable now. Their horses also wanted to follow us, so we took them. With the new rules now, where an accurate

Changing Times, Unrest, Taxes

account needed to be taken of everything we had, it was good to have extra.

We watched closely to see if the bandits followed, but they didn't. We weren't sure we'd seen the last of them though. They were likely to return for their horses.

We stayed in a small town that night, camping in the wagons to protect our valuables. The new families were encouraged to stay in the hotel. Our wagons were on the outside, with their wagons and the horses secured in the middle, including the bandits' horses.

That night, the bandits came for revenge. We had been taking turns watching for them. We spotted a man with a gun, and then four more. Nobody moved, while we waited to see if more would come. They were trying to figure out how to get their horses out. It would be impossible unless they hooked on a horse or two and pulled a wagon over. By now, there were a dozen bandits. We're in town and, with the new gun laws, we would have to leave fast.

The new travelers were plenty nervous from this afternoon, but we warned them they may have to dress fast to get out of town! The signal was given to fire, and we did. It was half dark, so we couldn't see how many got away, but there were nine on the ground.

Two of our guys ran to awaken the people in the hotel. Max's son was hitching a ride back and didn't have a bed roll, so he was in the hotel. It didn't take more than the first shot, and he knew what had happened. He sprang to his feet dressed from the day before, and rushed out the door with his pistol. Two groups of bandits were running past as he

Secret Death Defying Escape Finally Told

opened the door. One turned and fired, hitting Christian in the left arm. He returned fire, hitting the one who shot. He continued to urge people to run for the wagons. In short minutes, we're leaving. How badly was he injured? They washed the flesh wound and dressed it in the wagon. He insisted he was okay. We drove all day and set up again for the night. This time, we got a good night's sleep. Christians' arm was uncomfortable, but we would be there tomorrow. We arrived on schedule.

Christian's arm was treated at the clinic and he would be fine. Our new visitors didn't want to stay after these experiences! Nothing was said to the Russians that these people were Jewish. We thought it best to leave it unsaid.

Through the summer, more families came. We managed to accommodate everyone. They were all provided homes. Our newcomers fit in well because they're good workers. In addition, we have many other new neighbors too. Lots of Hutterites and Mennonites have been moving in around us. They are much like us in that they live in a commune setting. Each of us is independent, but the communes are community property.

They seem to have a religion of their own. The only person who conducts business, unless they delegate this to someone, is the manager. They are considered a sect. They're good neighbors, but I'm not sure how they will fare against the bandits. They don't believe in violence, and have never owned guns.

Many complaints have been sent to the government about the gun situation. They take our guns, but offer no protection. The Soviets are in one conflict after another, and our Hutterite and Mennonite neighbors are conscientious objectors. They do not take up arms under any conditions. It's hard to imagine how they can survive against the thieves and bandits. Besides, I can't see how the government, which is always short of able-bodied men, will put up with this viewpoint.

Max has been in Kiev for the last week, doing business and attending a hearing with the governor. He's probably the first settler to have a meeting with the governor! He has his records, showing our settlement's progress. We bring in more production, more taxes, and more stability than any other area in Russia. The governor was impressed, and promised to visit us and see for himself. They set up a time! Wonderful!

The reason for Max's visit was to show the need for guns and our own law enforcement. The new law disallows firearms but doesn't provide any protection to Russia's people. We needed permission to defend ourselves. The governor understood and gave us temporary permission to defend our gates, bank, stores, and people. He recommended we organize our own police force full-time and work with the government. Max was hesitant but agreed on a temporary basis. Max was concerned that if we were too enthusiastic and too skilled, they might send our people to quell other disturbances or even into battle. He was also angry that they had made him pay for poor quality Russian guns after the visit with the governor, when they still hadn't paid us for the guns they had taken.

Secret Death Defying Escape Finally Told

We had built a wall or stockade around our property, as had our neighbors across the road. We shared a road between us with no gates. Oftentimes travelers came at night, wanting food, a place to stay, and a store to purchase supplies from. The gates hadn't been needed until this time. Guard houses were built and strong gates erected. Men who had served in the Germany army were put in complete charge of our defense. They recruited 20 young men, who were given a salary and trained to shoot and defend our settlement. The guard houses were connected to the nearest house on either side of the gate, and all the businesses were connected except the mill and jail which was across the street. We were ready.

One day, when we were all at work readying our settlement for the governor's visit, an innocent-looking group of travelers came to one of the gates where several men were working, dismounted, quietly pulled their pistols out, and tied the men up. They proceeded to the store and then the bank. They knew just where to go, and they moved in quickly. As they entered the store, they slipped hoods over their heads and walked in. Albert's elderly mother and two employees were ordered to open the safe. Albert, who was in a back office, heard the commotion and pulled a lever to warn the workers in the bank. They slammed their door shut, warned the other businesses, and alerted the guards.

But it was too late for Albert's mother and the clerks. As soon as the safe was open, they were shot. Albert laid hidden behind his desk. They proceeded to the mill across the street. There, too, they killed six employees after taking the money in the safe. When the bandits saw the other busi-

Changing Times, Unrest, Taxes

nesses locked, they immediately remounted their horses and took off.

By this time, most of the settlers had been warned and were in hiding. But two 15-year-old girls were walking across the street when the bandits rode through and grabbed them. They scratched and fought, but were tossed onto the horses. The slight delay helped the settlers though. By this time their guns were ready, and they were soon blazing. Most of the riders fell, and as the remainder approached the gates, the guards there knocked them down. Several were wounded and were taken to our new jail — our first inmates. The doctors treated them there. The hoods were removed and the bandits identified. Government tax people! The tax people who spent several weeks here, and knew right where our valuables were! They didn't know about our warning system though, and didn't know about our guns. They were also taken by surprise by the determination and teamwork of our group. After interrogating them, we found out that they did this often and had always escaped, leaving no clue as to who they were.

It was a somber day. One of the original village builders and eight others had died. Grandma was 96. The funeral was held the next day. Max and Albert were sad, but they considered all here as brothers and sisters.

The next afternoon the governor and his entourage arrived. Max informed him of the tax collectors and their raid, and asked them to take their dead and wounded back with them. When the governor found out who they were, he was outraged. He knew them all and was informed that even those in his own office in Kiev had been involved in

Secret Death Defying Escape Finally Told

The Governor and his entourage arriving.

these raids. Max thanked him for giving the guns just the week before so they could protect themselves.

The governor was apologetic, and vowed to clean house. This was done immediately. Those who knew about the raids went to jail, and those actually involved were executed by a public shooting. He also offered jobs to any of the village's young people. Eight accepted his offer. Their ability to speak both German and Russian would be valuable in his office. He also knew they could be trusted.

Under the leadership of this governor, our villages prospered. He visited several times a year, staying in our guest houses, joining in feasts, and taking part in our evening dances. He always liked to take sausage and Kimmel home with him, and he brought us gifts and gave us many breaks. He told us that his state ranked among the best because of our contributions, and the colonies around us also prospered.

Always lurking in our minds, though, was the uncertainty of what would happen if the governor was replaced or

Changing Times, Unrest, Taxes

died, or if a new czar came into power. The older people especially seemed to want to go back to their homeland of Germany. So a meeting was held and those who wanted to leave were to inform Max by morning.

Max went to see the governor, and informed him that several older people wanted to return to die in Germany. He didn't mention the young people who were also planning to return. In checking with the neighboring colony, about 100 of the 300 families wanted to return and about 20 of our own families. We promised the governor that the land would be farmed the same as it had been, and the exodus would be kept as secret as possible. The governor would be in trouble if higher government officials found out he had given approval. He informed his special guards at the border to let us through, and he sent guards to protect us on our journey. He was truly our friend.

Max was now in his eighties, and his best friend and brother Albert was dead. He was no longer needed in Russia. His son Christian was managing the bank, another son was general manager of the store, and his daughter and Albert's daughter were married to brothers who operated the mill. The other businesses in town were owned by friends they had provided assistance to initially, but now they were doing fine.

So Max and his wife decided to go back to the fatherland to visit his father's grave, who was buried in a secluded part of Frankfurt. They had always been afraid of anti-semitism and of having their graves destroyed. Even though he had never known his father, he felt he had received inspiration and ambition from him.

Secret Death Defying Escape Finally Told

When they returned home, they visited the grave. Things in their hometown had changed. Very few friends still lived there. Many had gone on to America. Even those who had returned from Russia had then gone on to America. They decided to visit America themselves; they were still in good health. So they spent three months in America, visiting friends and family in Minnesota, Iowa, Nebraska, the Dakotas and Canada. They were totally impressed with what they saw, and couldn't wait to return to tell others — to encourage their children and grandchildren to go to America! America had everything — freedom of religion, prosperity, everything! They returned to Germany enthused to tell their news.

The return was a disappointing blow, the biggest Max had ever received. They couldn't see their family, or even send a message of any kind across country borders. New leaders had taken over, young men were drafted into the army, all ties had been cut to the West, no churches were allowed, and many restrictions were in place.

Max knelt down and prayed for a long time, thanking God for eighty years of blessing. He asked God to watch over his people awhile longer. He implored him to let them come home once more. He prayed over and over, spending each day walking and talking in low tones to his Lord.

Max's son, Christian, on the other hand, hadn't heard from his parents in over a year. He didn't even know they had traveled to America. The old governor at Kiev was still in charge, but didn't wield as much power anymore. Christian and his son, Daniel, went to see him. They said they wished to see what happened to his father, and asked permission to see him in Germany.

The governor conceded that he had little power anymore, but he would send a letter to the border and hope they would get through. The governor had sent a gift for the guards, and they smiled and sent us through after we signed a 30-day return.

The new regiment had brought in the Red Army and cleaned out the bandits for two hundred miles. They'd burned their shacks and made it safe for traveling. At least it was one decent thing they had done.

When we arrived in Germany, Max and his wife were so terribly happy. Everyone was crying with joy. Max feared he would never see his family whom he loved so much, ever again. We brought along Albert's wife who had stayed in Russia, Max's children and grandchildren, and a few special friends. After a 25-day reunion, we made plans to return.

Max did everything in his power to convince his family and friends to go straight to America. Christian felt we had to talk to the others and not run out on them. We loaded up on surplus cash, which we had done over the years during our trips to Germany, and headed back.

When we returned and told our friends what Max had told us, many more wanted to go. The question was how? and when? Armed guards were now placed all along the border to the west of us. No one was getting through. Some were content to stay in Russia; they thought this would all blow over.

Secret Death Defying Escape Finally Told

Christian and his family were determined to leave, but didn't want to risk any lives doing it. Some were slipping out alone and getting out. Some were getting caught and shot too. The colony to the south of us had two entire families killed just last night as they tried to leave. We debated leaving via the river that was between us and the guards. If we swam it, there would still be guards on the other side to sneak through. Also, with the border still two days and a night away, we would need more supplies than could be carried if they swam. It was too big a risk. We decided to wait a couple months until the river froze over, and then make our escape.

Christian's family prayed constantly that the Lord would show them the way out and let them be his disciples. They told no one of their plans, lest somebody inadvertently say the wrong thing.

By now, the Russians had built a large building about a mile east of us, and they had auditors, military men, tax people, etc., working and living there. They were in our settlement every day, auditing and snooping, making life miserable. Those who were planning to leave were packing quietly only their most important belongings, but everyone was quiet.

Amidst all of this tension, a rash of illness spread through the colony affecting mostly the children. The disease started with fever and pain, but in many cases, was also crippling the children. Christian's son August fell victim, and it left his left arm slightly crippled. Others were affected more seriously. The doctors had never seen or heard of this disease before. Dozens of people were ill at the same time. (Polio had struck.) The doctors felt these children needed to go to Germany for treatment.

Again we went to the governor and told him our plight. We suggested that if we left the area with the sick children, it may not spread any further into Russia. He agreed and said he would personally deliver a letter for our people. He assured us that we would have no problem. He arrived the next day, but stayed in their government building about a mile away. He was afraid of catching polio or carrying it to his family. Nonetheless, the letter came.

We saw a spark of good coming out of this tragedy. All of the children were readied to go unless the parents really objected. Many adults also wished to leave, and the Russians were anxious to have us out. Since our friendship circle now extended to our neighboring colony, we slipped those in who wanted to leave from that colony. We had quite a wagon train. Of course, many weren't ready to leave everything behind. The store, bank and mill had been sold to groups in the settlements who wanted to stay. They didn't have enough money to pay for all these businesses, but were given three years on the balance. Christian and Albert's son, Jake, stayed awhile longer to complete the paperwork on the sale. They did, however, send all their cash along to Germany.

When we arrived at the gate, the guards stood back and waved us through, never inspecting anything. They wanted nothing to do with us.

Secret Death Defying Escape Finally Told

When Christian and Jake's work was finished, they went to the authorities and showed them Daniel's arm. They agreed to let them leave, but stipulated that no one else could accompany them. The authorities now suspected that too many had gotten through the last time.

Christian's family began packing. Wooden trunks seemed to be the best way to pack their valuables. Furniture was taken apart and packed. Dishes were carefully protected and packed — what a job!

That night, there was a knock on the door. What a surprise! A small group from the colony had come with money — their payment on the businesses. What good timing! After we heard of their difficulties in getting it to us though, we wished they hadn't taken such risks. Christian's family said good-bye to the land that had become their home, and set out on a new journey.

The news from the colony is that they're being harassed more and more, almost like they're being smothered. The Russians will tell you quickly that they need the products raised there. The colonists now raise tobacco, beans, peas, sugar beets, soybeans, wheat, oats, meat and a tremendous amount of garden produce. These food products are shipped all over Russia. So Russia depends heavily on the colonists, yet they still harass them. They do pay well for their products anyway. The generation at the colony has changed completely now. The younger generation has never really seen anything but Russia, and they consider Russia their home.

The people of Jewish ancestry are still nervous, but are doing well financially and do enjoy farming and agriculture.

Changing Times, Unrest, Taxes

Their numbers have grown to more than 400. Jewish people are still arriving from Germany and have a complete city of their own a few miles away. There they can secretly practice their religion and keep their individuality.

Several Jewish people had a financial interest in buying the store, the mill and the bank from the Wolsky's. These people had been in business in Germany and were helpful in bringing new ideas into the businesses. They are hard workers and intuitive, often creating their own businesses.

From Max's and Albert's father on down the family lineage, none of the children were involved in farming and working fields. Instead they were managers, working equally long days to ensure that their own businesses were profitable and smoothly run.

I remember and knew my Grandfather Wolsky well. I was raised next door and spent a lot of time with him. I was just old enough to run and do the "gopher" jobs that he no longer could. He always wore a suit on the farm, when everyone else wore bib overalls. He wore the vest coat and all, with a gold watch on one side and a fob with a gold chain hanging across on the other side. He walked around to each of his fields each day to see how they were doing. He could tell you in what stage the grain was at all times. He could estimate, with amazing accuracy, the yield of a grain crop before it was harvested. He counted the stools (number of stems) on a plant and the number of kernels in a head to compute the yield in bushels of the crop. This provided him much valuable information — how much bin room he would need, how he wanted to blend, etc.

Secret Death Defying Escape Finally Told

Grandpa Daniel headed for North Dakota, where another family member had already homesteaded. The land homestead act was at its peak. My grandfather and great-grandfather homesteaded a quarter or 160 acres. The act specified that settlers had to build a house and establish themselves by a specified time. This they did.

Many ethnic groups did not understand farming, especially on the prairies of Dakota, and walked out. They were happy to sign quit claim deeds and go back east. Grandpa acquired some of this land and soon had a thousand acres, and was growing. He needed help, so he sent back for friends living in the east. He offered to pay their fare of $900 to get them here. They worked 13 months to pay it back. He eventually enticed about a dozen men here.

His crew also included two women to help grandma and to assist with the dozen children he had of his own. He kept buying land and soon had over 3,000 acres, and more than a hundred head of horses. Grandpa never went into the fields himself; he always wore a suit and vest, and served as manager.

He built a separate house for the hired men. They were allowed to leave when their ticket cost was covered, but none of them did unless they got married. During the winter when the workload lessened, he sent the men to school to learn to write English and learn math. Several of these men married teachers. Grandpa always helped them get started farming on their own.

The farm was like a bustling city at five o'clock in the morning. By the time the horses were fed and harnessed and

Changing Times, Unrest, Taxes

the men were eating breakfast, they had their assignments and were on their way.

By 1912, the Russian government had relaxed its visiting regulations. Grandpa wanted very much to go back. He put my father in charge and asked me to accompany him. Even though I was filling in and helping in many areas on the farm, I could also be spared. I was the happiest kid in Dakota! I was 16 at the time.

It was a long trip, but well worth it. We spent three months there in the summer. We heard sad stories of young men being badly treated in the army, many of who never returned, and of girls being raped by soldiers. People, in general though, were busy. The sentiment of the people toward the Russians was hatred. The Ukrainians and other colonists ganged together and told the czar they would revolt if he continued to interfere with them. By now, he had his hands full with a group called communists so, for the time being, he left them alone. These people had been lied to, robbed, pillaged, and taken advantage of in every way over the years, and they knew it would happen again.

While I was there, I had a wonderful time with the children I knew when I was small. I struck a special friendship with a girl, and we walked to all our old familiar places. I promised her that, someday, I would come back and take her to America. It was hard for me to leave.

When we had left Russia the first time, Grandpa Daniel had changed our name slightly — from Wolske to Wolsky. So when he wished to return to Russia for a visit, there was no problem.

Secret Death Defying Escape Finally Told

Shortly after we left, the visits stopped and letters quit coming. The revolution and slaughter had heated up. No communication. We had no idea how our family and friends were. All we had was hope and prayer. Grandpa and I knew that most of the people there were very religious. Each night, we would gather around and pray for their well-being. I could never get the plight of those people out of my mind.

CHAPTER 5

A Secret Mission

OUR FARMING operation was going well, and when I turned 18 my dad insisted that I attend college. North Dakota had an agricultural college in Fargo, so I enrolled there. I also signed up for their officer training program. One day, the commander called me in and asked, "Is it true that you can speak both German and Russian, along with English?" I answered yes, and explained my ancestral story. He was impressed.

A few days later, he stopped in with a high ranking officer and swore me to absolute secrecy. I obliged. They told me they were suspicious of what was happening in Russia and the many horror stories they were hearing. Yet they were unable to infiltrate the country to check it out. They had decided to send a handful of people to infiltrate as slaves in one of their Siberian slave labor camps. We would be equipped with cameras and small unsophisticated recording devices. We would be well equipped with many escape routes, friends along the way, etc. We would receive a full major rank and a $10,000 bonus if we completed our mission, and to our families if we did not make it. In addition, the government would pay for a full college education.

After much thought and prayer, I decided this was something I could do for the country who was giving us so much. Our assignment was top secret. My father only knew we would be on a secret assignment, but he didn't know where.

Secret Death Defying Escape Finally Told

I boarded a train at Fargo and headed for New York, together with a Major who knew his way around. There we met the other men, and spent a month studying maps, weather history, and letting our hair and beards grow. I learned to use a compass, and prepared physically like I had never done before with such activities as calisthenics and weight lifting. The other members of our group were professionals; they were military people. I was the only green horn. They had chosen me because I knew so much about the people, their languages, and customs. I was also much younger than the rest of them. In spite of this, they gave a lot of credence to my background and sort of put me in charge, which really puffed me up. Gave me a challenge!

When our preparation time was over, we were, once again, given the prerogative to continue on or stay. It was our choice. If we were successful, we had it made. If we were not successful, we would surely be executed. The people there needed help and food. The Russian government wanted a loan, and Congress wouldn't grant it until they had more information.

We all decided to go. The United States informed us that they could not admit they were involved. If we got caught, they would not admit they knew us. We were not to speak English, only German or Russian, depending on where we were. We were given pistols, not American made, but German. Our clothing was also German made. We were given a large amount of German and Russian money, and a small amount of Finnish and Polish money. We carried no identification.

A Secret Mission

When we got to the border, we met a man who provided us with transportation — three teams of horses and two wagons. The wagons looked old from the outside, but they were new, quality wagons. We were supposed to look like peasants. The sides of the wagons were quite high with a top to protect us from the rain and elements.

The shortest and nearest route was from Finland. One of the men spoke Finn well, and the rest of us could manage the language too. He was the only one who spoke while we were there. The Siberian camp we were to get into was almost straight across, but the terrain was true desolation. We were traveling above the tree line, so only a few months of the year are not winter.

The last instruction we were given was, "Don't trust anyone. These are very desperate people." Our supplies were covered and never left alone; we slept in the wagons. Occasionally someone would approach us on horseback and try to visit with us. We provided little information.

We had thin mattresses to lay on and plenty of covers, so nobody got sick. We had been given so many shots before we left that I didn't think we could get sick! The only thing we had for treating illness was a large first aid kit. We had plenty of their most common medicine — Vodka! When it was bitter cold, a glass of hot water with a shot of vodka really warmed me up. Grandpa always had homemade wine and beer, but no hard liquor. This was my first experience, so I was careful not to overdo it. Besides, I didn't like the taste, only the warm feeling.

Secret Death Defying Escape Finally Told

Water was our biggest worry, to make sure we had enough containers to water the horses each day. So far, we hadn't had any problems. There have been lots of streams and few people. At night, we pulled off far enough so we wouldn't be seen from the road. We had a goat tied behind and a young cow to give the appearance of peasants.

We didn't really trust our contacts in this country, but they all seemed to hate the Commies. They were poor, but nice. We only stopped about once each week. After all, we had to return this way when we leave and we may need them. Finally, after several weeks of traveling, we were within five miles of the slave camp. We met with our last and most important contact. We put our horses and wagons in the barns so they wouldn't be seen.

We took our pistols and technical equipment and, that night, set out walking toward the camp, not knowing what to expect. I started to wonder why I had left my comfortable college to come here and challenge murderers.

When we approached the gate, we could see to our surprise that there were no guards. We slipped in out of sight. Now we had to figure out how to assimilate with the people there, get the information our government wanted, and then get out.

At daybreak, the first group of about fifty men walked right by us. We were hidden. My God, we would have had to starve for a month before we would look that bad. We were fatter than the guards! They would absolutely spot us a block away. Now what should we do? Here comes another group, and they look even worse. About that time, I saw a

A Secret Mission

slave come out of the first house and join in walking with the second group. I figured that if he was a slave, he would be on their team. We decided to chance it, and see what was in the house.

We walked straight into the house like we lived there, opening the door and startling a woman so thin she could hardly stand in front of us. I asked her in German, "Are you German?" She said yes. We asked if she could hide us somewhere, and she showed us to the basement. There was a hole in the floor with a trap door in it, and a homemade ladder at the bottom. She told us her daughter was down there to the left, so be careful.

We couldn't believe the condition of the child! Nothing was left of her — starved to death. We gave them both some protein from our little packs, and even a taste of candy. We were afraid to give them too much or they would have gotten sick.

She said we'd be safe there until tonight when the men returned. The rest of the day we lay in the cellar, and I talked to the lady to find out what information I could. She was from the same commune area I had come from, and she told me that everyone was gone. This particular commune was almost all German Jew. One of their own people had gotten in trouble and offered to deal with the Russians — his freedom in exchange for information. But he said he hadn't expected anything like this! They tied him in the middle of the compound, so everyone could see and the authorities told the people that he was the one who squealed. All the townspeople denied they were Jewish, but they loaded them

Secret Death Defying Escape Finally Told

all into wagons and brought them here. There were only a few of the original colonists left. They didn't stop at that. They had been hauling the Germans out each week, making them work ten-hour days. They were fed a little cabbage soup and no meat for their rations. Each day as they died, their bodies were dumped into a pit and covered up. Who was the bastard who squealed? Arnold Schnell!

I knew him, but not well. Then she asked me, "Who are you?" I replied, "I'm Alex Schmitz." Her mouth opened in amazement; she put her arms around my neck, and said, "I'm Emma Klein." "You mean the Emma Klein I wanted to marry?" I couldn't believe it!

As I held her and many tears were shed, we finally began to talk. She said she had prayed by the hour that somehow God would intervene, and now He has. Then she said, "That's your little girl downstairs." I asked, "How can this be?" She said, "Remember how we used to talk and plan? You said you were coming back, and we took some chances. When I found out, I wrote many times, but no letters went through. I was able, with my mother and aunt, to have her at home, and we never told the authorities. They would have taken her away. We have been living on one ration between us. The soldiers will rape anyone. I don't see any of the little girls who came with us. I'm sure they're all dead."

She continued, "When all these things began happening, I got really nervous. I was afraid of what was going to happen. Jake had never been married, and was a nice man. If the Russians found out I was a single mother, they would take the baby and take me for their own purposes. I asked him if he would be my husband. I told him about you, and that if you should ever come back for me and still want me, then that's where I would go. He agreed and it saved both of us."

"Then the Commies came in and loaded up everybody. We wondered what we would do now. Jake pleaded with them to take his wife along. I guess they figured they could use me, and they have. To top all these problems, I have a tumor and it has all but consumed me. When I go, there is no doubt what will happen to Katrina. Jake will be moved to the barracks when I die. There are only a few shacks along here, and they are the ones where the wives are. The officers use these women as prostitutes."

Emma continued, "If their husbands object, they pull out their guns and the husbands disappear. As long as they don't resist, we can live. The lady next door has two babies — twins. I really fear for her. They have been especially hard on us because of our Jewish background. It's really pathetic! There are so few left. If we had only suspected and left when our brothers and sisters left ..."

"You begged me to go, and your grandfather even offered me a job. My grandmother was ill though, and I felt I must stay." Her voice faded away.

Now everything was becoming clear to me. I had prayed for several days before I made the decision to come, not knowing what magnet was drawing me here. Now I knew why. Our mission was inspired by God. I promised to take Katrina back to America with me, and give her the very best care I could. I would always tell her what a wonderful mother you were.

Secret Death Defying Escape Finally Told

In case the authorities challenged me about having Katrina with me, Emma signed a legal statement drawn up by Fritz granting me custody. We then went to the basement and told the others and Katrina about our connections. Katrina gave me a faint smile and a teeny hug.

We then sat down and began gathering names. Between Jake and Emma and a few of their real close friends, we got hundreds of names, stories and signed affidavits. We promised the people next door that they could go with us if they wished. Of course they were overjoyed at the possible chance for freedom. Emma approved, because she knew I would need help with Katrina. The men would check the place out that night. The Russians generally partied at night, so it should be quite easy to look around.

They said the guards usually went to their guard house and drank vodka, told stories, and laughed. We had to stay in the basement with Katrina who, in just a week, was showing great improvement and signs of recovery. Emma's health was deteriorating fast, but she was so happy. She was in immense pain, and until we arrived she had no pain killers. I marveled at the hell she had endured, mentally and physically, and yet she was rejoicing. She was thanking God all day long for sending us to rescue Katrina, and for having faith that we would all be united again. Today Emma has really weakened. She can no longer eat, and could barely stay awake. She told Katrina that God would soon take her home, and she would be waiting for the rest of us.

There were many tears and praying.

A Secret Mission

Something scary was happening though. The guards hadn't been real visible since we came here. Now we noticed a few guards standing around. They carried a jug, and it was obvious they weren't in much pain.

That night, four drunken officers came blasting through the door. They ordered Jake out of bed and they all began undressing. Emma started whimpering in fear. From the basement below, my anger was boiling. I couldn't take it. I asked my buddies, "If you guys want to help me, grab your pistols, shove them into their bellies and pull the trigger. That way it won't be noisy."

Quickly and quietly, we came up through the cellar hole in the adjacent room. They were all naked now, arguing who would be next. My three partners ran forward, shoved the guns into their naked bellies and pulled the triggers. I put the gun in the part that faced me of the officer on the bed, and all was silent. Poor Emma's heart could not handle all of this; she was gone.

We needed to get out fast now, but how? I apologized for losing my cool, but my partners agreed that we did what was needed. We took everything of value, and piled it up by the door.

Jake knew where everything was, so we harnessed the horses, hitched them to wagons, loaded them with supplies and feed, loaded our belongings, and sat down to determine our getaway plan. How could this all be happening? We drew a map of the layout of the camp, identifying the guard houses and the main gate on one end. We'd have to take care of the guards there as quietly as possible.

Secret Death Defying Escape Finally Told

Then Jake spoke up. He said, "Out of the thousands of German-Jews the Russians have enslaved, only a handful still survive. The rest have been buried in the trenches. Can't we somehow take the survivors along with us? If we can't, I will stay here. I can't leave them." We asked, "How many guard houses are there?" "Eight in all." "If we slip up to the ones at the gate and the two nearest to us, we can use our pistols, which are handier and quieter."

The lady with the little girls next door, came to stay with Katrina in the basement, and we all went out to look the situation over. The Commies were really celebrating tonight. I didn't know what the occasion was, but they all seemed to be in their quarters which were well lit up. Everything was falling into place.

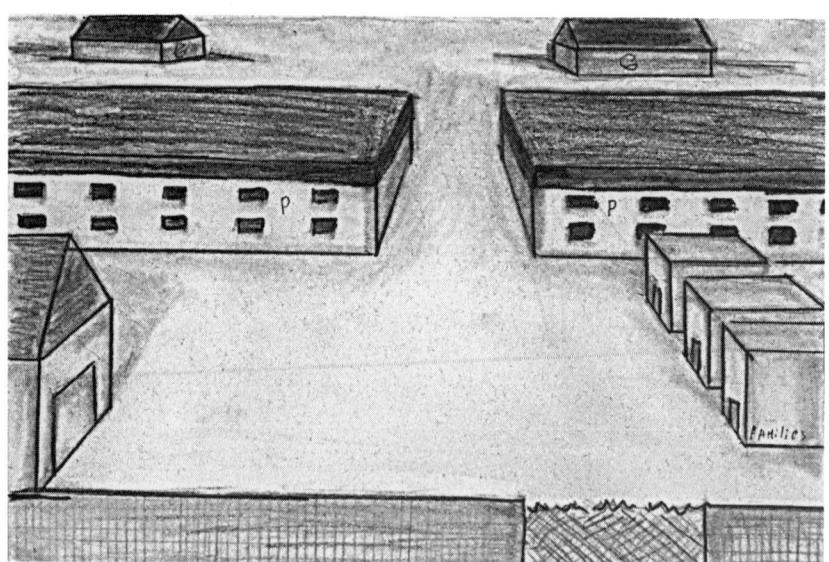

Prisoners were housed in large buildings. Smaller buildings were guard houses. Three small houses were for wives.

A Secret Mission

We split up, two at the front gate and the two closest houses. They were totally unprepared, and we took no prisoners. The block houses were about a block apart. We ran down the line quickly, afraid the others might have heard, but they were still drinking. We ran back and told Jake and his neighbor to run down the street to the barns to load the wagons and only their most valuable items, a blanket and clothing. We gave them one hour!

We went down the line and finished our job. Then we notified all the surviving prisoners. All came, although many had to be carried. They didn't want to die here.

I must stop and explain our reasons for being so ruthless. We weren't equipped to take guard prisoners with us. We had no idea what would lie ahead for us. None of this was planned; it just all happened. After all, these were not really humans. They were the lowest form of animals imaginable. Not a day went by that they didn't toss Germans and Jews into the pits dead or too dead to work or walk. They could have cared less. The atrocities the German Jews went through would fill too many pages to detail in this book. Those who lie in the pits did so solely because they were German or Jew. It was them or us ...

Secret Death Defying Escape Finally Told

CHAPTER **6**

Journey To Freedom

WE DECIDED TO FOLLOW the trail south out of here, and fast, and leave from where we had entered. It was only five miles to a safe place. Our contact had a well hidden farm, so if daylight caught up with us, at least we wouldn't be seen. The last thing we did before leaving was to torch the place. Everyone was nervous.

We pressed the horses on, faster than normal. As we approached the farm, something was wrong. No buildings. Everything was burned to the ground. Somebody must have alerted the authorities, and our contact person caught. That would explain why the guards seemed to be keeping a closer vigil at the gates a few nights ago. We didn't stop. It was a moonlit night, and we didn't disturb anyone.

We had no choice but to travel quickly now, and we did. We only went by one village, and they were not up yet, so I don't think we were noticed by anyone. We made 30 miles that day.

The next night, however, we pulled off out of sight. We had been traveling on a main road. Again we had to plan our strategy. We decided to split into three groups, so if we were caught, at least some should get through. Also, a smaller group of wagons would not be as noticeable.

One of the first problems we needed to deal with was lice. Head lice infected the people and they were awful.

Secret Death Defying Escape Finally Told

They bit, itched, gave the people sores, crawled on you, and infected them. They drove you buggy!

These people were covered and red with them. The Russians had done nothing for them — just laughed at them.

We felt sorry for the suffering people. One of the ladies came up with a concoction which was basically kerosene. You couldn't leave it on very long or it would burn your skin. So all heads were clipped with scissors and treated. After a few minutes the lice began to die. Then the head was washed with warm soapy water.

The treatment sounds easy, but we were in wagons fleeing from the Russian army. We were doing this as we moved. Everyone was naked and going through the process. What a process! It was repeated again in several days, because of any eggs that may have been embedded.

Their clothing was burned and, would you believe, after all these people had been through, they thanked us. They had the first night's sleep they'd had in weeks.

As I watched this torturous operation, I'm reminded of when I was a small boy in North Dakota and was sitting beside a slough. Off to my left I could see a red fox trotting toward the slough with a stick in its mouth. My eyes were fixed on him. When he reached the water, he was very close to me. I ducked low and he proceeded into the water, walking very slowly, stopping every little ways. Finally, all that could be seen was the very end of his nose and the stick in the air. He stayed in that position for awhile. He then let go of the stick and walked to the edge, shook himself off and

Journey To Freedom

trotted away. By this time, I had to see what he was carrying. Low and behold, the stick was covered with lice. Then I knew what he was doing — delousing himself. The lice, in order to avoid the water, took the last vestige — the stick — and he walked away clean. Too bad we can't get rid of them that easily here.

We took a head count and made some decisions. The dozen or so women and their husbands, if they had them, would go with Fritz and I in the smaller band. John and Yori would go down next to the tree line, so they could pull in and hide at night. They were, by far, the largest group. Theirs was the Lutheran group, 1,200 strong, and they had wanted to take this route.

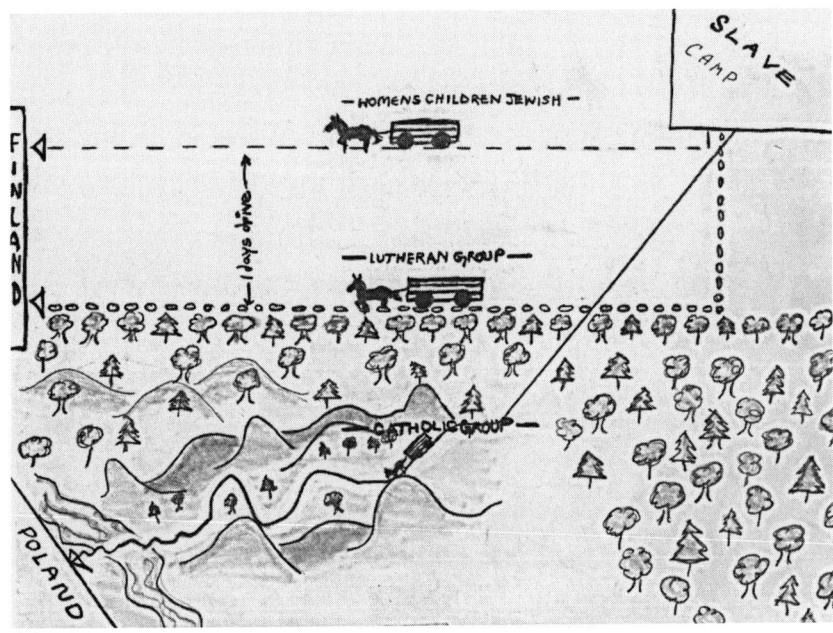

They were divided in three groups hoping at least one group would get through. Two groups were above the tree line, one went below it.

77

Secret Death Defying Escape Finally Told

The third group would cut southwest. They would not be able to use wagons until they got nearly out of Russia. They would have to have pack horses, and do a lot of walking. They had some riding horses and would have to take turns. This was the safest route as far as encountering Commies was concerned, but they faced other hazards. Lots of wet ground, almost no people or settlements in an emergency, and wolves were everywhere. It was more hilly too, but would be slightly warmer as they went. The Catholics were in this group.

The division seemed a natural one, as Lutherans and Catholics were not on the same terms as they are today. There was no more association with each other than necessary. There had already been a number of scrapes, and these people were weak to begin with. If they were stronger and in close quarters, I could see bigger problems. This group had about 150 men. The Catholics lived mostly to the south in the Crimea, and would be incarcerated in a different camp. We had enough problems without asking for trouble. Ed and Georgi led this group.

We had lots of guns and ammunition now, as we had confiscated all the soldiers' guns, several hundred in all. Yet none of these people knew how to use them. Only soldiers were allowed to have guns, so civilians had never learned how to use them. Yori and John chose a few of the stronger men and taught them how to shoot, without using ammunition. The guns were in the rear wagons, in the head wagons, and in the middle. This way, if we saw trouble coming from the rear, the wagons would continue while the rear ones would stop and handle it. Should they come from the front, the lead wagon would stop and the rest would follow suit. We would keep as many from getting hurt as possible. We were fortunate on another score. These wagons had been used to haul prisoners and supplies to the camps. But with so many buried and by winter perhaps the rest, these wagons would have been moved south for winter use very soon.

Everything has fallen into place so well. Everyone feels the whole plan is God's will. Open prayer and thankfulness abound throughout our groups all day long. People who are ill, frostbit, hands blue with pain, cry with happiness.

I know we are not all going to make it. They know that too. It's the kind of thankfulness and faith I'm sure God wanted to see. I just pray it will carry on through the years.

I've been debating what the bureaucrats in Washington will say when they are told about the wagon loads that are coming. Maybe they won't accept them. Then what? It's a bigger problem than I care to deal with. Pray and move on.

Fritz and I had about 15 women and about five husbands. Among this group was Katrina, of course, and Jake and the lady with the twins, whose name was Ida. What a Godsend she has been! Not only does she darn and knit all day, but she has taught all of the others to do the same, including the men. Those warm homemade socks are the only thing up here; it gives people something to do, and helps keep them warm. Katrina is a different person. She is thin, but has energy. She still naps a lot, and she still freezes

Secret Death Defying Escape Finally Told

easily. I wrap her in blankets at night, and she insists on sleeping with me. She's still a very scared little girl.

One of our problems is water for our horses. We have enough cans and one barrel for an extra day's supply, just in case we don't find water. We have to watch for ourselves too. John and Yori have the bigger problems. If we get some breaks in hunting and have excess meat, their group definitely can use our help. It's going to be a moonlit night, so we will move as far as we can tonight. On our way, we'll get the extra food to John and Yori.

All of the sudden, Fritz said, "Look over there! What do you see?" Corn shocks out in the field! We all ran out and

Typical wagon used to travel with. The stove and the extra height were important.

grabbed a bundle or two, and put them in the feed wagon. They may come in handy.

The wolves are following, which is a hazard when traveling at night. We have a couple goats with us and two cows, but they are put in the wagons at night or the wolves would have them instantly. Our group has about six children and 15 women.

Down at Yori and John's group next to the trees, they had to build a four-walled enclosure that they can take apart in the morning. The cows are kept here at night. The wolves try to kill grown cows. That's hungry! They have about ten cows there, and use the milk for lots of things — not just to drink, but for cheeses, and they let the cream come to the top and use it on bread or for cooking.

Jake has a cousin who lives about 30 miles down the road. We pushed the horses hard all night, until about five o'clock in the morning. It wasn't quite as far to his cousin's village as he had thought. Jake had only met him once, when his parents and he had visited there. They lived about a mile and a half from town.

No one seemed to be home, so we watered the horses, fed them, and put them in the barn. Jake and I had approached the house, but found no one. There was very little furniture. We wondered what was going on. We all went to the house, lit the fire, curled up on the floor, and sat watching the road. We knew somebody would come to milk the goats, but is it Jake's cousin? or is he dead?

About eight in the morning, we saw a man walking up the driveway. We awakened Jake, so we would know if the

Secret Death Defying Escape Finally Told

man was a friend or foe. It was his cousin and Jake remembered him.

We asked if we could stay a day or two to rest the children and the weaker adults. No one knew if we could trust him, until he started telling us about the Commies. They had come in the night and took all the young men they could find, his son included. He hadn't heard a word from him in two months. His son had a wife and little boy, so she begged us to move in to town. She was very afraid. I still come out to the farm every day. Jake's cousin is convinced that his son will never return, and he asked if he could come with us. We agreed on the condition that he tell no one.

We couldn't wait more than two days. We weren't sure where the Russian army was, but we knew they would be looking aggressively for us the minute they found out what had happened. We figured we had at least five or six days on them, and they didn't know which route we took. However, they will be able to travel much faster because they will be on horseback.

When we left this village, we took Jake's cousin and his wife, daughter-in-law and their children. We asked him if we could take his stoves with us. The women wanted kettles and dishes, so he said he'd catch up with us tonight with his wagon. Load whatever you want.

It has begun to snow and that's a bad omen. It will probably snow every day for awhile. Bad news.

We would have to move extra fast now, because once the snow deepened, we would have to move slower. Jake's cousin had two sleighs and since it was snowing, we left two wagons in exchange for the sleighs. Since the wagons had high sides and a wooden roof on the top, we set up the three stoves with stovepipes through the top. We had taken Jake's fuel supply.

In the supply boxes from the prison camp, there had been a lot of dry beans, peas, flour and more dry powdered milk — more than we would need.

John and Yori were leading the large group of about 1,200 people. We had devised a signal system between us for sending messages. We would use one of our brown and white horses or maybe both. They would do the same, as they too had spotted horses. We loaded down the two pack horses, and Fritz and Jake headed south. They traveled at good horseback speed and finally found them just as it was getting dark. They were much further south at this point than we had expected.

It's hard to believe how happy they were to see the food! They are on rations, and this would be enough for several days. They had shot two deer that came close enough, but with a crew like that it takes a lot of food.

It's really snowing. They have been busy winterizing their wagons too. They had stopped at an abandoned farm and taken boards from the barns, practically the whole shed! They built tops on their wagons, took horse feed and two stoves. They had quite a number of sick and weak people, so these people occupied the one warm sleigh. The other was used as a warming up sleigh. The sleighs had also been acquired from the abandoned farm.

Secret Death Defying Escape Finally Told

They also told us of one of their experiences. As they approached the tree line and headed west, people in the last wagon noticed something down the line. They decided to have a half dozen riders from one wagon hide in the trees to see if it was potentially dangerous. If it was serious, they would come back and get help.

It turned out to be only a half dozen wagons. But when they got closer, they noticed the lead wagon had eight Commy soldiers. The rear wagon was tied behind and held about a dozen prisoners. When they approached alongside, our men ordered the soldiers, "Hold up!" The Russians, who had been drinking vodka as usual, laughed at our boys. They fired and toppled the whole bunch. The prisoners and our riders finally got the wagons stopped, but one of the Commy soldiers was still alive and shot one of our men before they finished him.

The wagons didn't have a lot of food, but they were well supplied with blankets, two stoves, guns, boots, and most anything else they needed. The newly rescued prisoners were very happy to be with us. They told us the Commies were not going to send anymore prisoners north. They were needed south to finish a track of railroad and highway yet this fall.

That was good news to hear. There will be nobody, no communication at all for awhile. We may have gotten a week's head start, maybe longer.

The last wagon in the Commy group had been filled with vodka. This must have been the last vodka run of the year. The people were glad to have it, but they were warned not to overdo the drinking. I had never had an alcohol experience. At home we had homemade wine and beer, but only a glass. I had never gotten drunk with it. I was told a little shot of vodka in a glass of hot water really warms a person up. Most of these people drink it straight out of the bottle. John and Yori have some strict orders on this, and I'm sure they won't have any problems.

The tree line is a problem. Sometimes they have trouble getting all those wagons in. One advantage is that they have lots of fuel, and the trees provide a barrier from the wind at night. It is snowing almost all the time now, and it's fast becoming a problem.

In fact, late that afternoon, we spotted a village ahead. Yori and John did just what I would have done. After dark, they entered the village. John and York went door to door, offering to trade a wagon for a sleigh, ten dollars to boot. These people were happy to trade. Their sleighs weren't worth more than five dollars and they'd be getting a wagon. They had no trouble trading with them, and transferred their belongings to the sleighs. We didn't trade off the wagons with the guns; we didn't want them seen. They were able to buy three sleighs without a trade, so after we left the village, we transferred the guns. What a beautiful difference riding in a sleigh — smooth and the horses pulled so much easier.

Now back to our little band. That evening Katrina asked if her mother had died. I told her she had fallen asleep and went to God's arms. "She said to tell you she loved you and would be waiting for us to enter God's kingdom so we could

Secret Death Defying Escape Finally Told

be reunited again." Katrina said her mother had told her she was going to die because God wanted her back, but that he would find a way to take care of her, and He did. "He sent you, didn't he?"

Tears and a feeling of pride consumed me at the same time, along with a humbleness that is indescribable. Katrina had brought the same realization to me that had been reeling through my head many times. It was clear why I had chosen to leave a warm bed, a college campus, and the comforts of home for all the danger, misery and responsibility I had accepted here!

This was, without a doubt, directed by God. Again, I was not only humbled, but determined to give my life if need be to make this mission a success. Katrina still didn't want me out of her sight, and I didn't mind. I'm sure any three-year-old who went through what she had would also have a sense of insecurity.

By now, we have lost all communication with those who had sent us. We were presumed dead. With snow and winter upon us, our chances looked impossible. Our hope of getting out alive depended on God. And He had brought us this far. We were confident He'd bring us all the way.

We traveled by night when there was moonlight. We rotated the horses to keep them fresh. Jake's cousin had given us a couple barrels to fill with water in case we ran into an extremely dry area. We were living on the same food day after day, but nobody complained. Along with the dry beans, peas, milk and wheat, we shelled the cobs of corn we had picked, soaked it and cooked it. It was a tasty change.

Journey To Freedom

The change in Katrina is unbelievable. All the milk she could drink has made her healthy. We have three goats now and a young cow, who was severely attacked by a wolf last night. She doesn't produce a lot of milk, walking all day and being bothered by wolves at night. So we decided to butcher the cow that evening. It cooled out that night, and that first taste of meat was out of this world! The goats continued to milk well, in spite of all their walking. They were put in a sleigh at night away from the wolves.

Secret Death Defying Escape Finally Told

CHAPTER 7

The Ravages Of Winter

FARMS ARE GETTING FARTHER and farther apart. We don't see one now for several days, and the weather is getting much colder. We need to better prepare ourselves. Our wagons are in need of repair. In the next town is a man Jake knows, and he's sure he can be trusted. I hesitated to tell Jake that we didn't trust anyone; we were getting desperate. That afternoon, we arrived at his place. He didn't trust us too much either. As we expected, his place was very dirty. We didn't use his dishes or beds, and slept on the floor. It was infested with mice and rats.

We decided to keep an eye on him, but we never saw a gun. We noticed he had meat. We shared some of our rations with him, but we were running low ourselves. He seemed to appreciate what we did for him. I asked him what kind of meat he had. He said it was an older horse he had butchered. He offered us a chunk of horse meat, but I explained that we had just butchered a cow. We did accept some potatoes, carrots, and onion which he had a good supply of.

The next morning, I noticed he had a couple sleighs. I offered to trade two wagons and twenty dollars for the sleighs. He traveled by horseback in the winter anyway, and the sleighs hadn't been used for a couple years. He was happy to trade. He felt he got the better deal!

Secret Death Defying Escape Finally Told

We had confiscated some canvas along the way, so we made a frame around the sleighs and over the top to keep the elements out. Thanks to our knitting crew, we all have warm wool socks, mittens, and even some sweaters. We made holes through the canvas in a number of places to shoot out from, and also to watch for Commies or strangers. We had a stove bolted down in each sled. The women rode in one sleigh and the men in another. The sleigh was layered with heavy feather ticks covered on the top. Inside we were warm, but when you had to go to the bathroom, Wow! it was cold. The bathroom was outside, and we stopped periodically for that. The women had several five-gallon pails which they used in the sleigh.

The feather ticks we had were made from a heavy canvas-like material on top, and the bottom was filled with about six inches of goose and duck down, the really soft feathers. They are then stitched through every twelve inches to hold the feathers in place. These blankets were very light and very warm. They were all man size, about six feet wide, so four people could be covered with them at once. We had also nailed together a portable lean-to. This was placed against the sleigh at night for the horses, so the weather and the animals couldn't bother them.

Now with all the snow, the mountain lions and even bears were getting hungry. The wolves continued to prowl around us. One advantage with the snow is that we see game animals more easily — deer, caribou, rabbits, etc. The caribou migrate to the south now, where there are trees and grass to eat. We hope to get a chance to hunt them again when we are out of meat. We pray each night for our brothers who may be worse off than we.

We are ready to leave this morning. We painted our wagons and sleighs white so they will be more difficult to see in the snow. The old bachelor we had stayed with was going to help us, but he saw on the underside of a wagon board the words, "Property of Russian Army." He went a little berserk. "You have betrayed me! You are spies! You have come to kill me!" He couldn't be reasoned with. We tried to explain and tell him no, that wasn't true, but he threatened to report us. We wondered, now what? John went to the barn to hide his bridles, so he couldn't sneak off.

We decided to stay one more night. Maybe he would cool off and listen. Then out of the blue, he bolted for the barn. We were in hot pursuit, and Fritz was closing in on him. The old man ran to the first sleigh where we stored the guns. We hadn't shown him where they were, but he must have been snooping when we didn't see him. He grabbed a gun. I had stayed with Katrina, but my pistol was ready. They asked him to put down the gun, so we could talk. He ran toward us and fired. John went reeling. That was enough! They all fired; he fell dead. As it was, John's wound was superficial, though two inches further in and it would have been much worse. The women washed his flesh wound and treated it. I think John enjoyed the special care.

By the time we built a box to bury him, the excitement was over and two hours had passed. Fritz, who was a good Christian, read and prayed for the old man and asked for forgiveness. We pondered about the day's happenings,

Secret Death Defying Escape Finally Told

though things had probably worked out for the best. The old man was odd and we didn't trust him. Even Jake said he had changed. The Commies had treated him roughly.

We went into his house, took a stove, and decided to take another sled. We took horse feed, a extra harnesses, and two saddles. We harnessed the horses and hooked them to the extra sled. Fritz and several others wanted some of the pork, so they butchered it, cooked up the meat and left the rest for the cats. We put his goats with ours. The day was almost over, and we had to roll.

The wind was critical. When it comes, you are immovable. Most had been sleeping off and on during the day, so we were ready to make up some time. The horses were well fed and rested, and so were we. We traveled all night to make up time. We rested for awhile during the day, and kept going. We met two sleds today, the first we had seen.

Everyone stayed hidden except Fritz and me. Fritz could talk Finnish, but he acted like he couldn't understand them. Finally through gestures, they said in Russian, "A week away." Fritz pretended he couldn't understand them. They kept asking what we were carrying, but we kept going. We were ready to shoot, but we didn't have to. They didn't follow us. They were government hunters, shooting caribou, deer and reindeer. I think they would shoot anything that moved.

The weather has turned very cold — 30 below zero. The snow really creeks when we walk. The worst is when we stop for toilet time. The guys jump out; there's no visiting or reading the catalog. Wow! Do you move! I think that's where the saying "movement" began.

We had taken a lot of horse feed with us, at least ten days worth, but we were out of just about everything. We would have to raid the next village, somehow buy, trade, or whatever — we must have food.

That night, the horses put up a fuss. We knew something was wrong. We grabbed our guns and peered out of the holes. A herd of caribou or reindeer were crossing in front of our sleighs. We aimed and fired at the herds. We got four, but any that were wounded were quickly taken by the wolves or other predators following them. We happily took our four and butchered them on the spot. We did, of course, a fast job, but we must have gotten 800 pounds of meat. We began cooking it in our huge iron kettles. As soon as it was cooled out, we cut the rest into maybe 50-pound chunks, and put them in the supply sled to freeze.

This is a lot more meat than we will need, so we decided to head south to the large group on the tree line. They are parallel to us, but about a day south. We put about 100 pounds on each of two horses and two riders went south. Fritz and Jake left to deliver it. It was a day's ride down and a day's ride back, with maybe a rest day in between. They had one of our spotted horses, and we told them we'd somehow get food in the next town. Jake said the next town was a good sized town. May even have a government food dump.

Now let's catch up with the group way south in the woods with the pack horses.

Secret Death Defying Escape Finally Told

They normally traveled faster than the sleds, except the going wasn't easy with lots of trees, sloughs and hills. They sent two riders out ahead each day to sort out and find the best trail. They marked it similarly to a Boy Scout trail. They haven't encountered anyone until today. Four men were cutting trees. They spoke Polish and Russian, so that was no problem. They told us the wood was to be sold in town just over the hill.

We had a nice visit with them and found out the Russians raided them regularly. This was the Catholic group. There were several Polish people in this group who knew the way. You could not trust anyone, however.

They really needed a horse, as the Russians had taken theirs. We would trade a horse for a cow if we could butcher it right there, and just take the meat. They agreed to this. We then struck up the second bargain. We would give you another horse, if you give us four sleds and sets of harnesses. They were happy to, since nobody really had horses. We asked them not to say anything about our being there.

We had meat, bread and milk and were happy. It was obvious we were into a more civilized area, and several trails lead out from here. We figured we could get the sleds through okay.

It has become very cold again. Looks like they got the sleds just in time. Remember, these people had been sleeping in tents. This system had worked okay, but with all this snow and extreme cold, it could kill the weaker ones. This is all a Godsend. We prayed and gave thanks for coming to our rescue again.

The Ravages Of Winter

That evening, when it was dark, we hooked up the horses to the sleighs and took the trail they had told us was best. We did a little last minute trading — sugar for wheat, which we needed for cereal. The wheat was soaked overnight after it was washed. Then it was cooked until it cracked open and started getting mushy. With sugar or honey, cream or milk poured on it, it was a tasty healthy breakfast. When we were short of food as we are now sometimes, we would eat it three times a day. Together with a chunk of meat, we were happy!

Before we left, we built wooden tops on the sleighs and set up the stoves in them. Wood was not a problem around here, just the opposite of the land up north. We gave the Polish woodsmen a couple bottles of vodka and they were happy to help us with whatever we needed. We also gave them four old guns we had with ammunition, so they could shoot a deer for food. At the last minute, we told them what we were up to. They wanted to go along, but didn't want to leave their children.

We left about midnight with a parting drink. We got onto a good trail, leaving at midnight. We figured we'd draw less attention.

We made good time, except to stop for water and feed for man and beast. We traveled all night and all the next day. These people made a form of bread they called fry bread. They made the dough like they were going to make loaves, but then they fried it. Obviously there were no ovens aboard for baking. It tasted good, especially if you were really hungry. Anyway, while we were stopped, we made stew. The villagers had given us carrots and squash, so with the caribou

Secret Death Defying Escape Finally Told

meat, we ate heartily. We were bushed from the long drive, so we tried out our newly made beds in the wagons. The bottom half was hay, then feather ticks and blankets. Boy, did we sleep!

Even though we had pulled off into the trees that night, there was a lot more activity than we had seen since we started. You couldn't be careful enough. In Russia, even the children were taught to tell on their parents.

As we were rising the following morning to leave, a lone horseman came riding toward us. Ed and Georgi had their guns ready. As he got closer to us, we recognized him. It was Frank Sadek, one of the villagers we just left.

"Boy, am I glad I found you," he said. "The day after you left the Russians came on a raid. Took several men, our few animals we had left, and were about to leave when we ambushed them with the four guns you gave us. We got them all. Shot the Commies. There were four of them. Now we must all leave or they will slaughter us. Thank you for those old guns. We would have been kidnapped."

He directed us to go on a different trail from here, not as good but safer. He told us to stay on it for a day and we would come to a town. "If you stop outside the town in the trees, they won't see you. I will go with you. I have family and friends there, so if we want information on the Russians or anything else, I can get it. If we tie up here one more day, the rest of the villagers will catch up. There are 14 people." They knew every inch of this ground.

We did this and when we arrived, we really ate. They had

sauerkraut and sausage, chickens, geese and ducks. That may not sound like a big deal, but to the Germans, that's a holiday!

They had brought along everything that was important to them, even their livestock. They all wanted out. At this point, I wasn't sure how all was going to work, but all we could do was pray and try. When they found out we had guns, they feared no more. They arrived ahead of schedule, but we decided to stay overnight. Most of these people stayed in the village with the villagers they knew or were related to. I have an idea there was a party down there that night, because the next morning we had three more sleds of people with us. All of them came, and they brought a lot of good food also.

We noticed that the ratio of villagers was about four women to one man. The men have been nabbed. By dawn, we were on our way. Some of the women were weeping, but they knew they couldn't stay here. Soon they were talking about a new land, and were thanking God for their rescue.

The trail we were traveling was right next to the trees, not as good as where we had been, but safer. It's been snowing every day. It looks bad. The weather is about to get really mean, according to these folks. The only way you can move when those storms hit is by horseback. We would then be in big trouble. Our group was now 300 plus, with about 100 villagers. We must get through with the sleighs, or we can't move this many.

It had been snowing steadily for days. The snow was at

Secret Death Defying Escape Finally Told

least three feet deep, but it was loose, no wind in the trees. It was like in upper Michigan. Everyone, however, noticed the huge black cloud in the west. Bad news.

We went as long as we could, way into the night. The villagers knew of a place where there was water and good shelter. We put the sleds in a circle and shoved them tightly together so the animals could be let loose in the circle. The goats were put into a wagon, or the wolves would have had a feast.

The storm lasted four days. Ed and Georgi were not sure they would get out of there. The wind had never really gotten into the trees, so even though it was up the horses' bellies, they could walk in it because it was fluffy. We changed lead teams about every hour and let them go back toward the rear. The lead teams faced the worst of it as they had to break a trail.

We have had to butcher a beef and several lambs each day to feed all of these people. We knew they were running into big trouble with the bitter cold. The cold was affecting the horses and all of the people, some of whom have died. All prayed for a better life to come. They had been living in hell, and all had faith that God was guiding them. All prayed for their brothers and sisters in the other groups.

The weather is now in the 40 below range. This morning we had to shoot two horses which had gotten pneumonia.

According to these people, we are getting near the border, but the going is slow. We really must be careful now. Not only do they guard the border tightly, but there are many more travelers around. From now on, we have to go around villages because guards may live there and there may be too many questions to answer. We are not in the position to take on the Russian army or any part of it. A feeling of total faith pervades our group. The Lord will find a way.

We only dared to travel at night and get into the trees and hide during the daytime. We had several riders ahead a mile or so to check over the situation.

We just crossed over a major trail and we are told that it is near the border. We can't make it by morning though, so we must go as far as we can and find an especially good hiding place for today. Our riders have returned and tell us the line is within a mile. We must get in a good hiding place today. The horse riders scouted out the tree groves in different places. When they returned, they said we couldn't all fit into the same place. We'd have to split into two groups to hide. And we'd have to hurry; it was nearly sunrise. We just made it!

Our riders took three-hour shifts, watching all day so no one would surprise us. All went well. I don't think we were noticed. That evening, a half dozen of the guys who knew how to shoot went to the border. As they approached, they saw lights and a large group of men. There was a large building that appeared to be a mess hall, because the men went in and out regularly. Soon, less came out than went in. We approached on foot and soon, there was nobody outside. As we got closer, we could hear music like violins and accordions. Lots of laughing, so we knew they were into the vodka, as usual.

Secret Death Defying Escape Finally Told

We went back to our horses and rode about a half mile north of their building. There we found a good place to cross and a road that led straight back to the sleighs. We needed to leave immediately and as quietly as we had ever been in our lives. We moved now. Two riders rode ahead to warn us, but the coast was clear. Silently and quickly, we went with God's guidance.

CHAPTER 8

Freedom, Opportunity, Life!

WE TRAVELED STEADILY until midnight, not really believing we were free. By midnight, we stopped and rested, feeding the horses and ourselves. Many of our people were in pain and frostbit, but they were crying for joy. We will arrive at a large enough town in a day or so, and Georgi and Ed will make that phone call to the States and shock the pants off the "Brass" in Washington. I have no idea what their verdict will be, but we pray it's in the affirmative.

At least one group has made it!

They were hoping to find a Catholic church soon after they arrived to go to mass and tell God how thankful they were.

Meanwhile, Yori and John were having sleigh problems. Traveling in the trees had been hard on the sleighs. They had run over fallen trees and some rocks, and had breaks that needed fixing. The problems were fixable, but they had no real tools out there. We still have plenty of money left, so we decided to stop at the next village and see if we could buy some replacements. We are also desperately in need of more stoves. Many don't have them and it's terribly cold. This morning it was 40 below.

So we discussed our plight. There in a distance was a settlement, but it was not long before nightfall. We discussed

Secret Death Defying Escape Finally Told

our plan. If we saw a sled, we'd go to the house, and offer them a sled that needs fixing for a good one and $10.00. They should all jump at it.

The first one we came to said, "Go ahead. Take it. You have taken everything else." He thought we were the Red Army. We explained we were not, and told him of our offer. He grabbed it. "Most of us have no horses left," he said, "so the sleds are useless to us." He said the Commies were there last week and took their animals, so unless they can get some meat they will all starve. We told him we had a little reindeer meat, no real surplus, but we would share some with them.

I finally offered, "Look, we are going to Finland. Do some of you want to go along?" The whole village jumped at the chance — about fifty people. I told them we'd give them an hour to get their personal belongings together and be on board. They all had canned goods and vegetables, which they readily shared. These people know this country, and that'll be an advantage for us.

We now have a stove in every sleigh, a roof over the top, and a kettle of stew cooking in every pot. Every sleigh of people gave thanks before we started. This group, perhaps, had the toughest journey. They were sleeping on the wagon floor with no heat, and were running perilously close to running out of food quite often. They were the largest group, the Lutherans.

It took a lot of all types of food to feed 1,200 mouths off the land. Quite a few have died. I am reminded that many of these people were in bad health when they came aboard.

Freedom, Opportunity, Life!

I was quite sure at least half of these people would have been dead by now if they were still in the camp. But now they are on their way and are very thankful.

We traveled that day and half the night, hoping to catch up to Jake and the rest of our groups. They knew they had gotten behind. They stopped to rest and feed the horses, when the local villagers who had joined our group noticed the black clouds coming in from the west. "These are bad snowstorms," they told us. "These wagons may not be warm enough. The horses and animals won't be able to stand it. We must get inside soon." They said there was an abandoned settlement just ahead, which would be better than nothing. We agreed to settle in there for the storm. We told the men to hitch the horses back up and proceed a little further to get out of the storm.

We had a good shelter in the trees where we were, but these folks should know; this is their home. We hadn't gone very far, and we came upon the village. Unexpectedly, a woman came out and greeted us. We said we needed shelter from the storm. She said that only about half of the shacks were occupied. We found that the Russians had cleaned them out. The people who were here had left in such a hurry that they had left behind their canned goods, and even some of their chickens and goats. We gathered our newly acquired supplies and, together with our own, we thought we would have enough to make it.

We told the villagers we had our own food and would be happy to share, if we could stay overnight and wait out until the storm passed. They laughed and said our stay may be

Secret Death Defying Escape Finally Told

more like four days or all winter! They welcomed us. It would mean about 40 people per house, but many of the men preferred to sleep in the warmer looking barns. The horses, of course, warm the building a lot, and they took their blankets out there. Seventy-five percent of the people here are women, just a few older men. We lined up all the sleds in the most sheltered area.

All of the barns were connected to the houses with an underground tunnel. When the wind and weather was its coldest, a person couldn't breathe or stand outside. The tunnels allowed passageway for feeding the horses.

I'm not sure how all the people spent the night, but after four days there seemed to be many friendly pairs. I guess that's normal. I'd vouch there will be some wedding bells ringing if we ever get through this.

The Jewish people among us seem to stick together in their own group, but always volunteer to help in any way they can. They want to do more than their share really. They had been treated the roughest in the camp and had been there the longest. That's why there are so few left. They realize that none of them would be here today, if we hadn't come along. We get along fine with them. Most of their families are dead.

There are also a few Jews traveling with Alex and Fritz. They are praying as hard as we are.

It took a half day to get shoveled out and reloaded. These folks, like the others, also wanted to come along and we invited them to join us. It was slow, hard going now. The snow was deep and we know the horses are a big worry now.

Freedom, Opportunity, Life!

The four-day rest was a blessing in disguise. The horses got rested and well fed. It's going to be tough pulling from now on. I'm amazed how they can do it. Nothing left of them but skin and bone, but they are tough from working every day.

The storm would also hit Alex, Fritz and Jake. Let's see how they fared.

They saw the storm coming, but were in worse shape to deal with it than the Lutheran group. There was just no cover here. They had gone as far as they dared without finding cover. They would go over one more hill and if they saw nothing, they would head south to the tree line. At least they would have some cover. Lord willing, as they came over the crest, they saw a farm about a mile down the road. They had no choice. Friend of foe, they would have to get cover. This storm would be a killer.

When they arrived, the place looked abandoned. Fritz went to the door, but nobody answered. He called out in Russian first, saying "We are friends." No answer. Then in Finnish he repeated the same words. The door opened and a very large blonde lady opened the door. She said, "Are you Finnish?" Fritz stammered a little and said, "No, but I am not Russian. I am your friend." About that time, a little guy half her size came to the door.

They invited us in and we told them we would pay them or trade if we could put up our horses and stay here until the storm was over. They said the Russians had taken their animals, so they had no meat. We told them we would share our meat with them. We told them the whole story about

105

Secret Death Defying Escape Finally Told

our escape from the Siberian labor camps, and our hope to reach Finland and then the United States. "That's it!" the man yelled. And he hollered toward another room, and out came four of the prettiest and blondest girls, 17 to 20 years old. He said they had no choice, but if the weather would warm a little, they would put on their snowshoes and try to walk to Finland. They knew they would die here, so it was obvious they were glad to see us!

He showed us where he had built a false wall where the girls hid when the Russians or strangers came through. They, of course, went to town when they had business. But none of the family could read or write, and had never been to school. The house was as spotless as a hospital. He had welded heavy tin together with an acetylene welder and made a homemade tub. It had a drain hole under which he had a large pail. When the bath was over, he would toss the water out. This is the nearest resemblance to a bath tub I saw in Russia.

Nels and his large Finnish wife, and their four lovely, innocent daughters.

Freedom, Opportunity, Life!

The vodka was brought out and everything was going great. The house was full of people. Katrina, of course, took to the girls who were seventeen, eighteen, nineteen and twenty years old. But the older girls were more interested in the guys. They seemed pretty normal to me. They didn't look like they'd mind checking out why they were built the way they are, even though at this point, they were still innocent.

Each of the girls has been sidling up to a guy, and as the vodka loosens everyone up a bit, it looks like the old man may have to change his attitude. In fact, the old man passed out first. The mother informed her daughters, "You girls are on your own, but if anybody does that, the man better decide to marry you." This was understood.

We all enjoyed the good warm four nights. The storm was terrible; I couldn't even imagine anything so ferocious. There is no way we would have survived in the wagons.

John and Yori have been doing their best, but it's been a tough go. The snow is deep, and the sleds pull heavy. They send empty sleds out ahead to break the trail through the snow, but it's especially hard on the horses.

We were sure Jake and Fritz and the boys were waiting for us. At least we hoped they were. Evening is near, but still no sign of them. Wait a minute; here comes the spotted horses. It's Jake and Fritz, almost frozen. They were dressed super warm and covered with heavy blankets over their heads, just peeking out occasionally. They said we were close together, but they would wait until we showed up, hopefully in the morning.

Secret Death Defying Escape Finally Told

At five in the morning, we would leave. In a couple hours, we caught up with John and Yori. They had a huge breakfast cooking when we arrived. We gave the horses a two hour rest and fed them oats. Then we headed west with our fresh horses breaking the trail. A couple riders had gone on ahead to be certain there would be no slip-up. Only five miles to the border. Freedom for the most beat-up people in the world was a breath away! We just slid right in. The horses wanted to give up, but they didn't. They had unbelievable stamina. The heirs of these horses will surely be tough.

We still had to travel a ways before we got to a place where we could place a call, and we were eight to ten miles into Finland when we stopped at a village. This village was really too small to have even a telephone, but the trail is much better.

The people are very friendly and hate the Commies. It was good going now. Lots more traffic and well kept trails. It was obvious we were in a different country. We traveled another two days in this bitter cold weather. They told us we were about a day away from Helsinki. Another storm was brewing, and we wondered, "Would we make it?"

We decided to forge ahead and give it our best shot. Everyone ate, as did the horses, and we traveled steadily from about two in the morning until the next evening. We could see the outskirts of the city. The snow was coming down and the wind was picking up. We continued on and made it! In evaluating our journey, had we gotten caught out there, it would have been disaster.

Freedom, Opportunity, Life!

Again we all felt a heavy guidance, a safety net, that was with us this entire trip. The wind had died down when we entered the city. Jake knew where the capitol was, and I figured the U.S. Embassy must be close to the capitol, so we trudged there. We found the embassy. The building was supposed to be staffed twenty-four hours a day, so we rang bells and made noise until we awakened an unhappy man. When we told him who we were, he almost flipped. Yes, he had been alerted we were coming. When we told him how many had accompanied us, he almost flipped again! He got on the phone again, and I could tell he was catching hell for not being better prepared. Then I spoke to the ambassador and told him we were 1,500 strong. He said he'd have to make some arrangements and get back to us. In the meantime, we were to register the men into hotels and keep the horses out of sight, if possible. He warned us not to cause any more disturbance than necessary. Keep the men out of the bars.

He called back and told Fritz and me to stay at the embassy. The rest of the people were to be checked into hotels. In three days, a ship would pick up everyone. The embassy staff would direct them to the ship. Fritz and I were to board a different Navy boat. The people treated us like kings. I was confident the Russians couldn't implicate the United States in any way. We had never spoken English in all these months.

Yori, Fritz, John and I stayed in the embassy, and of course, Katrina. Early in the morning, Washington officials were on the line. No one was 100 percent happy; they were

Secret Death Defying Escape Finally Told

mostly overwhelmed. They had agreed to accept all the immigrants. All were taken quietly to a Canadian port, and then to America from there.

We were told to buy two sets of clothing and shoes for everyone — and whatever else they needed. Charge it to the embassy. All were to get cleaned up and ready. Imagine how much water they must have used! Wow, were they happy! Two months ago, these people were skin and bones slaves. By this time, they would have all perished. Now they are alive and headed for the land of opportunity. New clothes, three meals a day... They have thanked God many times and have promised to help others and explain what God has done for them.

Nels, his big, wonderful wife, Jake and the lady at the camp with the twins were given the horses and the sleighs. They were worth a great deal of money, and when some were sold, they bought a piece of land out of town a few miles and started breeding horses. This will be a special breed of horses. All four daughters were married that day, and boarded the ship to America. A number of others also married — a happy group on their way to a new land!

The next day, the many wagons carried them to the ship and on their way. Nels and Jake received payment for using their horses and sleighs to take their friends to the boat. They were already in business. I had requested at least two doctors on the ship, because of all the frostbite and health problems the people had encountered.

Freedom, Opportunity, Life!

This ship was already loaded with refugees from Georgi and Ed's group. Another happy reunion! And they were on their way!

The seven of us, John, Georgi, Fritz, Yori, Ed, Alex and Katrina boarded the Navy ship which would arrive in the States in about two and a half weeks. The other boat would require an additional week.

We were picked up at the dock and taken to a big building where we met the commanding general. We were wined and dined for several days. Like the General spoke of our journey, "It's like seeing your mother-in-law go over a cliff in your new Cadillac. We're absolutely ecstatic with what you did, but international conditions are such now that we cannot recognize you publicly. We can't admit to anything."

I don't think any of us are worried. Receiving a major's uniform, a few other amenities, and money would be what we expected. No problem.

The general said he received permission from Canada to dock the boat at a Canadian port, and then have the immigrants board trains and send them to Winnipeg. From there, they can choose where to go. Some have family in Canada, but most headed for the Dakotas, Minnesota and Nebraska. The plan was to assimilate them into the population. President Wilson authorized $1,000 cash for each person. That's probably like $50,000 in today's money. Low interest loans were also made available so they could buy livestock and machinery.

Secret Death Defying Escape Finally Told

CHAPTER 9

German-Russians In America

THIS GROUP OF PEOPLE has been an important part of the development of some of the finest farmland in North America. The western half of the States are mostly livestock.

North Dakota raises more sunflowers, barley, flax, hard spring wheat, and sugar beets than any other state. There are more millionaires per capita than any other state. I believe the influence of the Germans from Russia has had much to do with this. Yes, it is a hardy climate and this alone requires tenacity and toughness. This was easy for the German Russians. They had never had it so good. Most had large families and expanded their farmland according to the amount of help they had. There were twelve on my mother's side and twelve on my dad's side, just like many other families. Many ethnic groups homesteaded land, though others didn't. Many didn't know a horse from a cow. They just wanted the free land. Unfortunately, farming doesn't work that way.

The homesteaders had to "prove up" their land. This meant building living quarters and a well. When winter hit many of these people in the face with 30 below zero weather, they wanted out! That's where the real tough ones came in. These folks offered quit claim deeds to those who could pick them up. This would void their obligation to the gov-

Secret Death Defying Escape Finally Told

ernment. However those who took over the deed generally received at least part of a house, a well and a few improvements. Often they would settle for $100 or less. My grandfather acquired a number of these. There was, of course, homestead land available, but this was limited to 160 acres.

Not all the German people in the Dakotas saw Russia, as many came directly from Germany. However, most are Germans from Russia.

The majority of the German Jewish people went into business in the cities — Fargo, Minneapolis, Chicago. Valley City had a German Jewish family, who my father would visit when traveling to Bismarck or Aberdeen. They, too, can be proud of the job they have done. The crime rate among these Germans is among the lowest in the country. Welfare is unheard of. Its people boast a high level of accomplishment.

At first when the Germans came, their children didn't have to worry about finding a job. They worked hard until they got married, and they got a farm of their own, often a piece of the home place. They always received a few horses and cows from home, and so did the woman as a dowry. The crops they raised were in high demand and so was the price, a gravy train for those who took advantage of it.

Most often, because travel was by horse, a courting couple didn't live more than a few miles apart. Quite likely, they met each other in church. Because language was sometimes a barrier, ethnic groups tended to live in clusters and formed their own church affiliations. As land became more scarce, more people learned English, and children went to school, the people too started spreading around.

The Scandinavians were the largest group in North Dakota by a large margin. They were Lutheran, but not the same affiliation as the Germans, so they each had their own church. Many times the churches were next door to each other, but the parishioners acted as though they were unrelated groups. Today with the exodus in progress in the Midwest churches, Lutheran churches have combined on a national level, with the exception of Missouri Synod and a few smaller branches.

Today's residents can't afford to pay or support a pastor in each building in many cases, so they are being forced to combine. In the sparse areas of the Dakotas, the handful of members don't want to give up the church their forefathers built, who now lie in the cemetery behind the church. So the Lutheran church has offered a Pastoral Assistant's Program for parishioners who wish to take over the duties as permitted by the church. They do this for much less money, in some cases only gas money, but this has allowed church doors to stay open. If the dedication is there, I'm sure there will be many great presenters and caring people in these positions. Church and faith have never left these people. God's hands are still strong, alive and working!

The Catholic group assimilated in the same way. At first there was tension between Lutherans and Catholics. Today, I believe, that has subsided. Intermarriages are common, and both the priest and Lutheran pastors are a part of the service. The Catholic church, too, has faced the same prob-

Secret Death Defying Escape Finally Told

lems of people leaving the state. One priest today often serves several parishes too.

The largest population group to settle in the Dakotas initially was the Scandinavians, most of whom came from Norway. They were not used to big farming, since Norway had small farms with limited farmable land. They adjusted well to the climate, and they were able to make a suitable living here, which continues today.

Today the largest segment is German, and their large families may have had some influence in this transition. South Dakota had a similar experience. In addition to Germans from Russia, the Hutterites and Mennonites also moved to South Dakota on an individual basis. South Dakota has more lenient schooling laws, and this was especially desirable for them. A teacher is allowed to teach at the colony, and their children attend their own schools. South Dakota has about 300 colonies, with about 300 people per colony. Some laws have apparently changed, and now North Dakota, Canada, Montana and other states also have colonies. These people are aggressive farmers and have prospered. I visited the original Hutterite colony near Vermillion, South Dakota. They still have the original Bible written 450 years ago. The cover is made from wood and it was written with a feather. Very unique.

In traveling the states many times, I have visited these people and done business with them. They are slow to trust a stranger. I find that if I speak German, their acceptance of me changes.

German-Russians In America

Years ago, the Germans were reluctant to store their money in a bank. In doing business with them, I often receive cash, and on one occasion, I received two pails of silver dollars. Couldn't even lift them! That was years ago, of course. Today the younger generation uses banks, but I'll bet they prefer a banker who is German.

The German still hold to many of the older traditions, such as dancing. Older music is their favorite. Lawrence Welk is a prime example. His music is still popular, and he was born and raised in Strasburg, North Dakota. Even today, when wedding dances are held in Strasburg, the whole family, including smaller children, are allowed to dance. Weddings are an important celebration; divorces are looked down upon.

Crime among the Germans is very low. They don't consider it a problem to have a drink or two or a beer. I have seen much less drunkenness. In looking back at Nels and his beautiful blond daughters, they all married their man and are still married. They all raised fine families and even their grandchildren are blond.

Katrina turned out to be a lovely, wonderful girl. Of course, I'm not prejudiced! She has excelled in art, and has sold thousands of dollars worth. Her beautiful paintings are exhibited in classy galleries. After nearly starving to death, she came back beautifully, though she has had a few health problems likely as a result of that time. She says it's nothing serious. She has been the apple of my eye. She married a man who plays violin in the philharmonic. They have two children and live in New York. he is Jewish, which would

Secret Death Defying Escape Finally Told

have made her mother very happy. They return every summer; she paints and the children run and play. North Dakota has an active Germans from Russia organization, holding regular meetings.

By 1917 it was obvious we were being drawn into war. We faced the first draft conscription this country had ever had. We were headed for war. The people out here had seen enough bloodshed and hardship, but if drafted, they were prepared to go. The Mennonites and Hutterites were always conscientious objectors. They served as medics, suppliers, etc. Along with the war came the worst flu epidemic in history. Whole families were wiped out. More people died (12 percent) than at any time in history. We did not go to town for weeks, but got along with what we had. We raised huge gardens and literally lived off the land. We cooked wheat from the granary as cereal, and it was good. Years later, we learned this cereal was also healthy for us. When the mailman brought mail, we put it in the oven and heated it as high as we dared without damaging it. This was done to kill germs. None of us ever got sick. Wheat soared to eight dollars a bushel. Farmers were rich. All the land was grabbed up.

There were no synagogues here at the time. There were Lutheran and Catholic churches popping up all over. I think some of the Jewish people married into other religions, and may have gotten swallowed up. This, I believe, is one reason most of the Jewish moved to larger cities where they could practice their own religion. Their mark on America still continues. Many have given large endowments to schools. I have known some personally, and America is better off for them. Even though the number who returned with us was few, the trip was worth every bit of sorrow we all went through. This whole scenario could not be made public before, because of the tension between the countries. Some of the families in Russia, and perhaps in this country, could have been in jeopardy. It's only now after fifty years that we dare.

Secret Death Defying Escape Finally Told

CHAPTER **10**

A Wolsky Family Overview

MY FATHER, Melvin Wolsky, who farmed our land before me, planted many apple trees and evergreens so we are really nestled in here. I, too, have planted fruit trees and we love a large garden. Many deer and wildlife visit our yard regularly. It's sort of a haven for them in harsh weather.

The house I live in is not the original house, which was only three rooms. Grandpa and Grandma raised twelve children here, so in 1906 built this large house.

At first, only grandpa, his father Ludwig, his mother and two sisters lived here. One sister, Susan, married Fred Utke and one sister married Adolph Kurtz. They all had land close together and farmed and raised large families.

A son of the Kurtz's, Herman, lived next to us all of his life. He had two sons, Harold and Raymond, who are still neighbors.

The Utkes also had a large family, but most of them also have left this area. Irvin Utke has several boys in the area, Danny and David, Jerry Utke of Enderlin, and Herbert Utke family of Oriska.

I have lost track of most of the women. Mrs. Leroy Butke still lives on a farm near Lucca, and Mrs. Elmer Geske lives in Enderlin. Mrs. Walter Fraase's family still live near

Secret Death Defying Escape Finally Told

Buffalo, North Dakota. Her two sons are retired, one a lawyer in Bismarck and one in Fargo.

The Wolsky's are in many states, even though some are old. My father is 95 and still reads a book a day. His brother, Emil, is about 90. An aunt, Easter Richmond, from Portland, Oregon, is about 89. A brother, Leo, in California is near 80, and an aunt, Alice Befm of Illinois, is also near 80. The other seven have died; all had children. There are dozens of cousins and family members I have never met, but hope to in the future.

I have two brothers, Wesley of Nome, Melroy of Oriska, and a sister, Beatrice Peterson, from Oriska, North Dakota.

My grandfather, Daniel, farmed near Nome with his parents. His mother lived to be 96 and I knew her well. She was a small, gnarled little oak tree, never ill and always busy until the day she died.

Grandpa married Emma Tontoe, whose family had lived ten miles south and two miles west of Harvey, North Dakota. There were five in that family and her father died. Her mother remarried Gottlieb Fraedrick, who originally came from the Enderlin-Sheldon area. They had, I believe, three more children. Gerhard still lives near Goodrich, North Dakota. His brother John just passed away. Her youngest daughter Tonie just died in December. Tonie Blackway lived in Fargo and was 98 years old. She had a nice family. Dorothy spent her life in Africa in the mission field. Ralph is a printer in Fargo, Sidney a college professor, and Tom Blackway a well-known businessman in Fargo, North Dakota.

A Wolsky Family Overview

Martha, another sister, lived around Harvey, North Dakota. She married a man by the name of Bunns. I'm sure there were more, but I only knew two boys, Clarence and Liman. One has a daughter in California; one has a daughter who is a nun at Maryville, a place close to where I live. I don't know the rest of the children.

Johanna Wutzke had married Alfred Wutzke and lived in the Goodrich area. I believe there are still a son and daughter in the area. They have a son, I believe, at Verndale, Minnesota, who moved to California where they also have several children.

Bertha married Jake Wutzke, a brother of Alfred. She is the best known because she lived 60 miles from the closest doctor — in the "boonies." Many people couldn't or wouldn't go on a path with no road and with no decent vehicle to look for a doctor. Aunt Bertha had a special touch and helped many people get through illness or childbirth. She had a number of children. Rueben of Coolidge, Arizona, is the only one I know.

My grandmother, who was Emma, was very young when she married grandpa. I believe she was 16 years old and he was 35. I don't know to this day how or where they met. They raised 12 children and she always had at least a dozen hired men around to cook for. That was a lot to manage. She did so though, and lived to be 86 years old. She never sat around and talked to me like grandpa did. As a kid, I couldn't understand that, but now I can. I lived with her a few months while attending college, and when she had time to talk she was very interesting.

Secret Death Defying Escape Finally Told

I remember her telling about going to Harvey with her dad and they had to always be sure they left town so they could make it home in daylight because of the wolves. Even in daylight, the wolves would follow them and when their sled would slide down steep hills, the wolves would come right up close as though they were going to jump into the sled. Her dad was always concerned so he would whip the horses downhill to get a distance. The wolves never bothered them, but as a young girl, she was very scared.

She also tells of each of the children having a job to do beginning as very young children. Hers was official bread maker. Every day, many loaves had to be made for this very large family. There were several Native Americans living in the area at the time, and her father got along fine with them. In fact, they brought furs to him at times, and he gave them food in the winter when they were hungry. Something they really enjoyed was bread. One day, when she was home alone making bread and had just finished, several Native Americans walked in. They didn't knock, and she was in total shock. All they wanted was bread. They took it all, left some furs on the kitchen floor, and left.

She was afraid her parents would be angry because now they had no bread, so she started another batch. When they all came home, she told them what happened and her parents were so glad she was okay and proud of her that they let her go to bed and her mother finished the batch.

My mother's name was Ussatis, which I understand has a Lithuanian spelling. Many Germans went to the Baltic area (Lithuania) and settled, but they received such bad

A Wolsky Family Overview

treatment early on that they soon left and went to other areas. They were on rented land and could never buy it. They were also cheated on and treated poorly by their land.lords. The harsh treatment drove them out.

They went on down to Koigsberg (East Prussia) and then to Nikolaivka, and then to Kiev. Four children were born there and then they came to America, where they had a grand total of twelve children. My mother was the third oldest. She was born in Kiev. I have many relatives in the area from the Ussatis family.

My mother was taken home by the Lord in 1980. She was a kind person of strong faith.

The Ussatis family has done a fine job of keeping family roots and heritage together. A great-grandson of Grandfather Albert, Rany Peterson, did a superb job of collecting information and writing it.

My wife's name is Menge and they also came from the same area in the Ukraine. Her mother's family name is Lindeman, also from that area originally. There still are Menges and Lindemans in the area.

My wife, Dolores, was the third oldest in a family of nine children. Four sisters and one brother are still living.

Dolores and I raised four sons of whom we are very proud. They have never given us a problem, all graduated from at least one college and have been successful in their ventures. Our eldest son, Reg, has a very successful insurance agency. Steve, who also was in insurance sales, died two years ago at age 40. A horrible experience. Greg is an attor-

Secret Death Defying Escape Finally Told

ney and father of our special grandson, Alex. And Mark is a paralegal in Burbank, California. We love them all.

As I peruse the many telephone books here before me, and I observe the names, I recognize many whose ancestry are Germans from Russia. Many are here because a secret mission turned in their forefathers' favor, and they were rescued from certain death. They were then taken to the United States. This mission was kept secret for nearly one hundred years. Perhaps it shouldn't be told yet, but I feel people have a right to know their roots and future generations too would not be kept in the dark.

Sometimes severe measures had to be taken, but please remember, this was life or death. Certain death if they were caught. So rather than criticize these people, have empathy and forgiveness as you read. This heroic escape had to have been directed by God.

This is a novel based on history and actual accounts by my grandfather, who was there and told it to me. Germans from Russia have a unique background.

If you enjoy this book, please tell others or tell me.

Old German colonies in the Ukraine.

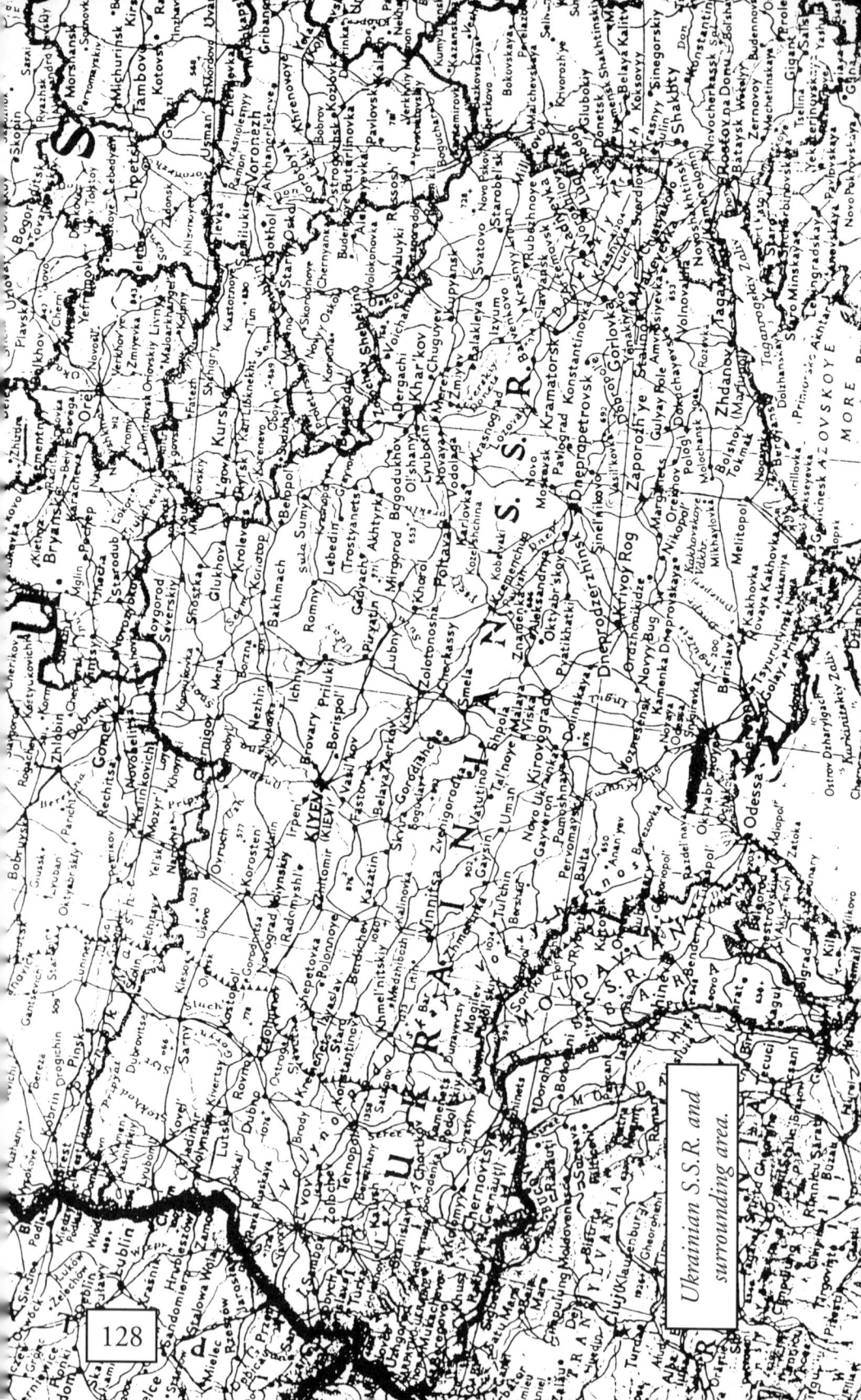
Ukrainian S.S.R. and surrounding area.

Eureka, South Dakota, was one of the largest grain handling stations in America.

Great grandfather Ludwig on Main Street of Fingal, North Dakota (3½ miles from home).

My uncle's original home as he grew up on the prairie.

Rural school on the prairie of the Midwest.

The Lawrence Welk farm as it is today.

The author with his 95 year old uncle, Gideon Klien, who was a business man in Eureka, South Dakota.

Grandfather and grandmother, Danial and Emma Wolsky.

Mother's wedding picture.

Father's wedding picture.

"The Beginning of a Bad Time" – The economic crash had come beginning the dust bowl on treeless North Dakota.

The Wolsky house as it looks today. (Built in 1906)

My father (95 years old) at his retirement home in Oakes, North Dakota with my cousin Gary Wolsky.

Uncle Gideon and daughter, Mary Ellen.

Old stone Mennonite church, Casselton, ND.

Ukrainian church today.

Rural church at McGregor, North Dakota.

Filmore Lutheran Church, one of the oldest churches, near Enderlin, North Dakota.

Seventh Day Adventist Church at Butte, North Dakota.

An old Catholic church in Butte, North Dakota.

St. Paul's Lutheran Church in Butte, North Dakota.

One of the very early higher education institutions as it looks today.